W9-DES-335

EASY OUT

Steven Sandor

James Lorimer & Company Ltd., Publishers
Toronto

James Lorimer & Company Ltd., Publishers acknowledges funding support from the Ontario Arts Council (OAC), an agency of the Government of Ontario. We acknowledge the support of the Canada Council for the Arts, which last year invested $153 million to bring the arts to Canadians throughout the country. This project has been made possible in part by the Government of Canada and with the support of Ontario Creates.

Cover design: Gwen North
Cover image: Shutterstock

Library and Archives Canada Cataloguing in Publication

Title: Easy out / Steven Sandor.

Names: Sandor, Steven, 1971- author.

Series: Sports stories.

Description: Series statement: Sports stories

Identifiers: Canadiana (print) 20190186488 | Canadiana (ebook) 20190186496 | ISBN 9781459414884 (softcover) | ISBN 9781459414891 (EPUB)

Classification: LCC PS8637.A547 E27 2020 | DDC jC813/.6—dc23

Published by:
James Lorimer &
Company Ltd., Publishers
117 Peter Street, Suite 304
Toronto, ON, Canada
M5V 0M3
www.lorimer.ca

Distributed in Canada by:
Formac Lorimer Books
5502 Atlantic Street
Halifax, NS, Canada
B3H 1G4

Distributed in the US by:
Lerner Publisher Services
1251 Washington Ave. N.
Minneapolis, MN, USA
55401
www.lernerbooks.com

Printed and bound in Canada.
Manufactured by Marquis in Montmagny, Quebec in December 2019.
Job #181187

Contents

THE END OF SUMMER

The ground ball skipped once, twice, three times on the red shale.

The shortstop for the Fort Saskatchewan Red Sox reached his glove down between his bent legs. But he didn't get down quite far enough. The ball skipped under his glove and between his feet. It rolled through the infield and onto the outfield, where it disappeared in the thick, green grass.

Mo Montpetit saw his chance. He'd been standing on second base, but now was sprinting toward third. The Fort Saskatchewan centre fielder tried to find the ball in an outfield that looked like it hadn't been mowed all summer. As the outfielder reached down into the grass for the ball, he stirred a swarm of mosquitoes that began to attack his delicious arm.

"Go, go, go!" the third-base coach for Mo's Westlock team yelled, waving his arm in a circle. Mo didn't slow down as he got to third. He rounded the bag and headed for home.

The centre fielder, fighting through the mosquitoes, fired the ball as hard as he could toward the infield. It got nowhere near the target, the catcher at home plate. Instead, it bounced a couple of times between the pitcher's mound and the first-base line before rolling off the infield.

Mo ran down the baseline and stomped his right foot on the plate.

"Safe!" cried the umpire. Mo's teammates streamed out of the third-base dugout for a group hug. His best friend, Remi Richard, smacked Mo on the batting helmet.

"That's the game! The winning run! We walked it off!" cried Remi.

But the celebration was cut short by the home-plate umpire.

"Okay, everyone, that's the game!" he said. "We're running late! We need both teams to quickly shake hands and then clean out those dugouts. We have the teams waiting behind us to play the third-place game!"

"Well, we got to celebrate a little bit," Mo said to Remi. They stood in line, waiting to shake hands with the Fort Saskatchewan players. "I mean, winning the fifth-place game is something, at least."

"Sure, fifth place in single A, tier four provincials," said Remi. "Our names will forever be remembered in the history of Westlock sports. The team that got a participation ribbon in a tier three levels below the top division in A-ball. I mean, move over Red Lions. Move over Legionnaires. The Westlock single-A under-13s will forever be hailed for not finishing last at provincials!"

"Hey, it wasn't that bad a season," Mo said. "I mean, we won about as many as we lost, didn't we?"

"Sure, but who's counting?" asked Remi. "This is A-ball. No pressure at this level."

"My dad's been saying there's big plans for next season," said Mo. "Or something like that."

"Yeah, whatever," said Remi. "Big plans might mean that they'll put new shale down at the diamond. Who knows?"

The Westlock players got in line, and sprinted through the handshakes and mumbles of "good game" with the Fort Saskatchewan players.

And with that, the single-A season was done. No trophies, no medals. Just a rush to get the gloves and bats packed into the baseball bags, then a dash to the parking lot for the long drive home.

1 Look Out, BARRHEAD

I know how I'm going to make millions of dollars, thought Mo. He dropped his shoulders and pushed a silver train of shopping carts through the slush-covered parking lot. *I am going to invent a smart shopping cart. When you're done, it drives itself back into the store.*

He waited for the automatic doors to slide open. There was a problem with the sensors that his dad had told him over and over he'd get fixed. Until that happened, a person had to stand in front of them for a couple of seconds before they'd open.

Mo pushed the train of carts back into the store.

"Excuse me, Mrs. Clements," he said to a woman carrying two plastic bags filled with groceries.

"Morning, Little Mo," she said. "Beautiful day, isn't it? Maybe we'll be lucky and it won't snow again. Wouldn't that be wonderful?"

Mo stopped pushing and nodded. "Yes, ma'am. We're all kind of hoping for an early spring." He tried to force a smile.

"Make small talk with the customers," his dad kept telling him. "Make them feel like they're family." But, wow, was it ever hard when they all called him "Little" Mo. They'd been calling him that ever since he could remember. *I'm in junior high, it's time for it to stop*, thought Mo. *But who am I kidding? They'll call me Little Mo when I'm fifty.*

"So, Little Mo, are you going to try out for the baseball team?" Mrs. Clements asked. She smiled so big that her lips pulled back from her yellow teeth. "I think it's just wonderful that they're bringing big-time ball back to town."

"Maybe," Mo shrugged. "Uh, Mrs. Clements, I have to get these carts back inside the store . . ."

"Oh, you go on," she said. "But I would have thought you'd be the first one signed up for the new ball team. You know, because of your father and all."

Mo just shrugged. He crouched down and pushed hard to get the shopping-cart train moving again. As he walked into Westlock Independent Grocers, he passed right by the same community notice board that adorns the front entrance of grocery stores everywhere. There were notices for babysitting services, pickup trucks and farm equipment for sale. Smack dab in the middle:

WESTLOCK IS
BRINGING AA REP BALL BACK TO
TOWN!

TRYOUTS FOR THE U13 TEAM — APRIL 4 AT KELLER FIELD! (R. F. STAPLES SCHOOL IN CASE OF RAIN OR SNOW AND/OR SUBZERO TEMPERATURES.)

Mo parked the train of carts inside the front entrance, then walked into the store. His dad, known around town as Big Mo to Mo's Little Mo, was in the produce aisle. He was arranging apples into a neat pyramid. Mo's dad wore a bright green shirt with a WESTLOCK INDEPENDENT GROCERS logo above the front pocket. Just like his son wore. Except, on his dad's shirt, underneath the logo, was the word "MANAGER."

"Saw you talking to Mrs. Clements out there," his dad said. "Everything all right?"

"Sure, she just wanted to talk about the double-A team."

"Ha," his dad smiled. "I think everyone knows you're going to ace this."

"I'm not so sure, Dad. I mean, we barely had enough players for our A team last year. And, well, I wasn't sure we were all that great."

"You won a few games," his dad said. "All of you were just getting your feet wet."

"Now we're going to put a team in the double-A league, instead? That's a big step up. I mean, we won games because a lot of the teams we played made as many mistakes as we did. And no one threw as hard as I hear the kids in double A throw."

"It is a big step," his dad said. He looked away from his son and at the Westlock baseball jerseys that were pinned to a wall behind the cash registers. "But you know that in this town, baseball was once top of the heap, right? I mean, senior teams, junior teams — we were all feared. The question wasn't *if* we'd beat Barrhead, it was by how much. And then, of course . . ."

"That provincial championship," Mo interrupted. "Dad, I've heard it so many times. I know. We all know. I mean, the older customers bring it up with you like it happened yesterday. But I'm not sure I'm as good as you were."

"Well, I guess we'll find out this year!" his dad said. "Follow me, son."

The two walked into an aisle filled with boxes of cookies and bags of potato chips. A worker was filling the shelves.

"Make sure to get that display of chips refilled," his dad told the worker. Then he turned back to his son. "Look, the fact that this town hasn't had a double-A team is pretty sad. We've got to get back there. Barrhead has a team in double A. And if they have one, we need to have one."

"Dad, why is everyone your age obsessed with this Barrhead thing? Whenever we go there, I think it looks a lot like Westlock."

"Bite your tongue, boy."

"And don't a lot of our customers make the drive here from Barrhead?"

"Some do, I guess," his dad smiled. "Look, they're fine people. But when we play against each other, whether it's ball or hockey or, well, rock, paper, scissors, *it's on*. And we're going to have a team that will go toe-to-toe with the Barrhead Orioles this year. Just like we used to."

2 First TRYOUT

Mo skidded his bike to a stop in front of the bike rack. Another bike followed close behind.

Both riders locked their bikes. They adjusted the packs on their backs. Each pack had the handle of a baseball bat sticking out of it like some sort of silver antenna. The riders took off their bike helmets and replaced them with faded Blue Jays caps. The morning snow had melted, filling the walk leading into the high school with brown slush puddles.

"I guess we're in the gym," said Remi to Mo as they pushed through the front doors of the school.

In the foyer, Mo and Remi slipped off their grubby outdoor shoes. They replaced them with clean runners they pulled from their backpacks. They walked toward the gym and pushed open the doors.

A man stood by a bucket filled with orange balls. They were about the same size as baseballs, but soft. The man had on a blue cap with a plain red W on the front.

"I recognize that cap," Mo whispered to Remi. "It's the Westlock Legionnaires cap from when they won the provincial championship way back when."

The man in the cap cleared his throat. "Little Mo, Remi, good to see you. I guess you guys are the first ones here."

"Hey there, Mr. Bilodeau," said Mo. "I didn't know you'd be coaching."

Joe Bilodeau sold pickup trucks at the dealership out on Highway 44. He had sold a new half-ton to Mo's dad the year before. Remi's mom and dad had bought their trucks from Joe, too. Joe Bilodeau's car dealership may have been the only one in Canada that didn't sell any actual cars.

"How's your dad?" the coach asked Mo. "I haven't been by the supermarket this week. Everything good?"

"Same as always, Mr. Bilodeau," Mo replied.

"Well, good to see you're following in your dad's footsteps," said Mr. Bilodeau. "We'll see if you can do what he could do on the diamond back in the day. I mean, we wouldn't have won that provincial championship without him. Oh, and one other thing, Mo. You can call me Coach B."

"Okay, Coach B."

Mo thought about how glad he was that his dad wasn't there. He had to supervise a produce shipment, so he wasn't able to come to the first tryout with his son.

First Tryout

Whenever Dad and Mr. B. get together, they talk about that provincial championship over and over. They'll never get over that Barrhead game, thought Mo.

"Did I ever tell you about the time Big Mo drove me home in our last at-bat against Barrhead?" Coach B. reached into the bucket. He tossed an orange ball into the air and caught it with his bare hand. "I mean, Barrhead's pitcher was Stevie Schaffrick! The Fireballer! He was a legend. And your dad, well, it was crazy . . ."

Fouled off three pitches, thought Mo.

"He had two strikes on him and Schaffrick kept pouring it on. Big Mo fouled off three pitches in a row to stay alive."

Then a pitch nearly hit him.

"Then Schaffrick wastes one inside, nearly takes your dad's head off!"

Then dad hits it to the fence, everyone scores and Westlock's off to provincials.

"Then, he comes in with the next pitch and *pow*! Your dad smacks it to the fence. I mean, if the wind hadn't been blowing in, it might have gone straight out! In any case, we all get around the bases, and we walked it off. A win over Barrhead! I still have problems selling trucks to people from Barrhead. They remember!"

★ ★ ★

Twenty minutes later, the clock on the gym wall let everyone know that the first tryout was supposed to have begun fifteen minutes ago. But Coach B. was still out in the hallway. Ten other kids, most of them wearing Toronto Blue Jays shirts, joined Mo and Remi in the gym. Mo recognized most of them from his A team. But there were a couple of new faces.

Another minute went by. Then another.

"What's the holdup?" asked one of the kids. "I want to be out of here and playing Fortnite a bit later!"

"I think the coach is waiting for more kids to come," said another.

Finally, Coach B. walked in. A few parents trailed behind him. The parents sat on the benches that stretched along the gym walls.

"Where's your dad?" Remi asked Mo. "I thought he was Mr. Baseball in this town."

"He said he'd be here in a while," Mo replied. "There's a big delivery coming in to the store today, and he has to be there when it arrives."

"Well," Remi said. "It's not like you'd need his help or anything. With your name alone, you'll make this team."

"Remi, look around," Mo hissed. "There are twelve of us here. Just twelve. I think *everyone* is making the team."

Coach B. leaned over his bag and pulled out a clipboard.

First Tryout

"Okay, everyone," Coach B. said. "I guess this is it for the first tryout. I'll be going through a few simple drills that will let me see your throwing, fielding and batting skills. I'll be making grades, just for my reference, on how you do."

Coach B. grabbed a soft orange ball from the bucket. "Line up along the wall there. Gloves on, please. First kid, please come to the centre of the gym. When I say go, you're going to turn away from me and run to the far side of the gym. When I tell you to turn, please turn and catch the ball."

The first one up was Sonia Semeniuk. Mo recognized her from school. Sonia was the only girl at the tryout.

"Go!" yelled Coach B. Sonia began to run and, as she moved, the coach lobbed the orange ball into the air.

"Turn!" the coach yelled, as the ball descended toward the player. As Sonia spun, the ball came down right at her. She had just a second to react and catch the ball.

The ball bounced off the outside of her black baseball glove.

"Don't give up on it!" yelled the coach. "Get it and throw it back to me."

Sonia scampered after the bouncing orange ball. She retrieved it and threw it — way over the coach's head. It struck the wall at the other end of the gym.

"Sorry," Sonia said. "This is my first time playing baseball on a real team."

Remi whispered in Mo's ear. "Judging by the number of players, she could make it. And then what? She'll be learning how to play the game in rep."

That's a scary thing, Mo thought. *I mean, I'm scared, and I at least played single-A ball last year. I can't imagine being a beginner and having to learn how to hit and field while playing against teams with top players on them.*

The next person went. He dropped the ball. Then the next. A drop. Then another drop. Then almost a catch. The ball bobbled in his glove, but slid out. Another kid fell as he spun around, and the ball dropped harmlessly by his side.

Then it was Remi's turn. The ball was up in the air. Remi turned and stabbed into the air with his glove. The ball disappeared inside of the leather fingers. He'd made the catch!

"Now make the throw!" yelled the coach.

Remi turned and threw. The ball bounced four times before it got to the coach.

"Great glove, no arm!" yelled the coach.

3 Dropping THE BALL

Mo was the last one to do the drill. As he got ready to begin his sprint, he saw his dad walk in. He was wearing a blue cap with red W, like the one Coach B. wore. He waved to the coach.

"Just in time, Big Mo!" Coach B. yelled. He turned his attention back to the tryout. "Now, go, Little Mo!"

Mo sprinted. There were goosebumps on the back of his neck. He knew the ball was already in the air.

"Turn!"

Mo spun and looked up. His eyes were filled with yellow and purple spots from the bright gym lights. He put his glove in the air. The ball struck him in the mouth and bounced away.

"Come on, Mo! Lucky that's just a soft practice ball! If that had been a real baseball, that would have taken out some teeth." It wasn't Coach B.'s voice. Mo knew it was his dad, because his dad was the only adult in town who didn't use "Little" in front of Mo's name. If his dad was really mad, he called him

Maurice. Mo always knew he was in trouble when he heard his full name.

The group of twelve did the drill again. This time, about half of them caught the ball. Mo wasn't one of them. Then they went a third time. Mo could feel his dad's eyes on him. He thought about how easily he caught the ball when they played catch in the backyard.

"Turn!"

This time, Mo caught sight of the orange ball right away. He put up his glove. The ball was headed right for the webbing. Mo squeezed. He'd caught it! But wait! What was that sound? *Thock! Thock! Thock-thock-thock!* It was the sound of the ball bouncing away. Panicked, Mo opened his glove. There was no ball there.

He heard his dad laughing. He was talking to the other parents. "The kid's nervous, that's all. He'll be fine. He makes these plays all the time when we're playing catch."

But, while his dad spoke, Mo could feel his eyes drilling two tiny holes right through his son's head.

★ ★ ★

The next afternoon, Mo couldn't help but think about that morning's breakfast discussion.

When Dad said: "Mo, how come you struggled to hit the ball at the tryout? You know you have to move your hands quicker!"

Dropping the Ball

When Dad said: "Mo, how come you threw so many balls away? You know how to move your feet. Rotate! Move your hips!"

When Dad said: "I know it's just the first tryout, but we both know you can do a lot better."

And then, the killer. This one his dad said to his mom, but Mo knew it was meant for his ears: "So I talked to Coach after practice and he thinks they're only going to get twelve kids in total. That's it for the tryouts. So everyone is gonna make the double-A team, no matter how they do over the next couple of weeks."

Mo's mom pulled the car over the curb. The morning had brought another spring downpour, so Mo was getting a ride to school.

"You shouldn't worry so much about your dad," she said. "All he wants is to see you succeed."

"Sure, by doing everything he did," Mo sighed as he climbed out of the car. "Later, Mom!"

Mo walked into the school and spotted Remi in the hallway.

"Hey there," Remi said, looking up from his phone screen. "All hail the son of a town legend!"

"Stop it, Remi." Mo shook his head.

"Well, didn't you see the notice on the bulletin board?"

"No," said Mo. "I just walked in, doofus. I haven't had a chance to look at the bulletin board. I mean, what's the news? Westlock is going to make a bid for a Major League Baseball team, now?"

Remi snickered. "Walk with me. Find out for yourself!"

Mo followed his friend down the hallway to the notice board by the main office. There, in the corner:

MAY BASEBALL FESTIVAL IN WESTLOCK
MAY 10 — CELEBRATING THE AA HOME
OPENER!
AA BASEBALL ACTION AND A REUNION
TO END ALL REUNIONS! WE CELEBRATE
THE 25th ANNIVERSARY OF THE
WESTLOCK LEGIONNAIRES PROVINCIAL
CHAMPIONSHIP!
WE ARE BRINGING THE ALUMNI BACK!
JOIN US FOR A CELEBRATION OF THE
BOYS OF SUMMER, IN THE SPRING!

Mo felt the blood leave his cheeks. His dad hadn't mentioned this to him!

"Oh, no," Mo said. "They're going to bring the old team together?"

"That's right," said Remi. "Coach B. and Big Mo and all of the legends whose names are up on the outfield fence. I think the whole town is going to get together and burn a Barrhead Orioles jersey at home plate."

"I mean, what is with this Barrhead hangup?" muttered Mo. "It's just a town down the highway from us. But talk to my dad and he makes it sound like something from a horror movie."

"My uncle and dad go on about it, too," Remi smiled. "My mom just rolls her eyes when she hears all the Richard boys talk about it. Barrhead versus Westlock. Westlock versus Barrhead."

Remi adjusted his cap. It was yellow and had a black P on it. Mo was pretty sure it was a Pittsburgh Pirates cap, but it didn't look like one he'd seen on TV. A perfect chance to change the subject.

"So," said Mo. "What's on your head today, Baseball Hall of Fame?"

Hall of Fame was what Mo sometimes called Remi, because of his friend's love of collecting all things related to baseball. *Sometimes I think my dad would like having Remi for a son better than he likes me*, Mo thought.

"Pirates cap, 1971 World Series edition. When they had Roberto Clemente."

"Who?"

"One of their best players of all time. He died in a plane crash after they won the World Series."

Oh, why did I ask? Mo thought. *We make fun of the Westlock old-timers. But Remi is just as bad when it comes to his caps and his baseball shirts and his baseball cards. One day he's wearing a Dodgers hat, but from when they played in Brooklyn. Then he's telling me about the Jays winning the 1992 World Series, like either of us was alive to see it. I guess we all have to love something. I just wish I loved ball as much as Dad and Remi do.*

4 In the CAGE

At least it had stopped raining. But it was still a cold, late April evening. The wind blew across Keller Field.

The baseball field was located in Mountie Park, on the western edge of Westlock. Mo thought that Westlock never grew, unlike other places, so the park would always be at the end of the town. To the right were the railroad tracks, where a train always seemed to be parked, blocking the crossing. Mo's dad often joked that the slow trains were a good thing, because they prevented people from leaving town and heading down the highway toward Barrhead.

Right behind Keller Field were the rodeo grounds.

The green outfield fence was decorated with retired numbers: 13, 11, 40, 22. There was a 4 in the right-field corner.

Mo's dad sat in the white stands behind the home-plate backstop. He was surrounded by a group of parents, huddled over coffees that were getting cold awfully fast. The twelve players were on the field, all with jackets on. Some wore their caps over their tuques.

"Okay," Coach B. said, as a vapour cloud escaped from between his lips. "It's pretty cold. But I need us to head to the batting cage over there. I need to see you take some swings."

"All right, Mo!" Mo's dad called from the stands. "Show 'em what you got."

The cage was located just outside the diamond. Coach B. walked in. There was already a bucket of baseballs sitting behind the screen. Coach B. went behind the screen, which left just a little bit of room for him to throw a pitch toward the plate. The rest of his body was protected from any line drives that might be hit back at him.

"First batter!" he yelled. "Come on, Remi!"

Remi had taken off his baseball cap (a 1981 Philadelphia Phillies replica) and replaced it with a black batting helmet. He grasped his orange aluminum bat as he walked through the gate and into the cage. He closed the gate behind him.

The coach's first pitch whizzed by.

"Come on, Remi! Swing the bat!" Coach B. called.

Remi shook his head. "That pitch was too high."

"Hey, we're not calling balls and strikes in the batting cage! Not every pitch is gonna be perfect. Swing!"

Remi took a mighty swing at the next pitch. It was

almost by him before he brought the bat through the strike zone. He whiffed. Then he whiffed again.

But on the next try, the ball came off Remi's aluminium bat with a sharp PING! It bounced on the ground until it hit the screen. The next pitch, Remi fouled off to the side.

"Okay, you're getting the timing down," said Coach B. "This is double A we're talking about. You're going to be facing some kids who throw pretty hard. I heard there's a pitcher from the Morinville Brewers who throws sixty miles an hour."

"I heard there's a pitcher from Barrhead who throws two hundred miles an hour and has three heads and six arms," called Mark Laboucaine. His long shock of red hair was barely contained by a too-tight Blue Jays cap.

"Okay, enough with the smart talk," said Coach B. He got ready to pitch again.

Watching from the dugout, Mo gulped. He thought back to A-ball the year before. He would sometimes have trouble hitting pitches, even though they were basically lobbed toward the plate.

No one in A-ball threw sixty miles an hour, he thought. He imagined how fast sixty miles an hour was. Was it as fast as his dad's truck on the highway?

The next pitch to Remi was high. Too high. But Remi swung. The pitch was in his eyes, so he had to raise his bat high and swing downward to make contact.

"You really tomahawked that swing," the coach said. "But at least you made contact."

Uh-oh, Mo thought.

Remi put down his bat.

"Sorry, Coach," he called. "I am finished *tomahawking*. Now I'll go do a little war dance for everyone."

"Oh, wait, sorry," Coach B. gasped. "I mean . . . but . . . tomahawking is a term for swinging down on a baseball. We say that all the time."

"Yep," Remi said. "I mean, you *could* have said, 'You swung down on the baseball.' But tomahawking is so much more, you know, *descriptive*."

Before he had met Remi, Mo hadn't really known what being Métis meant. Remi had moved into town from a farm in the county, and before that, *Métis* was a word that Mo had heard on the news or in class but hadn't really understood.

"My mother's side is . . . Indigenous," Remi had told him when they had first started hanging out. "When I was growing up it meant half-Indian or part-native or sort of-First Nations. Now we're all supposed to say Indigenous."

Remi walked out of the cage. In a quiet voice, Coach B. asked for the next batter to come forward.

Remi stood next to Mo. He whispered, "With just twelve of us, Coach knows he can't cut me just because I speak up. This might be fun."

Easy Out

When it was Sonia Semeniuk's turn to bat, she took a mighty swing. The bat flew out of her hands.

"Um, Sonia?" said Coach B. "Let's keep two hands on the bat through the swing, okay?"

Sonia nodded. She crouched low, her feet wide apart, as she held the bat in the air.

"Um, Sonia?" said Coach B. again. "Your feet are really, really far apart. A stance that wide will slow down your swing. Try to keep your feet inside your shoulders."

"But I watched a game on TV last night," said Sonia. "The best hitter on the Blue Jays has a stance like this."

Coach B. drew in a breath. "That's a player who has years of experience. He can do things like that because, well, he's a pro. But you have to play by the rules before you break them. Sometimes, watching big-league players isn't the best way to learn."

"He had three base hits last night," Sonia pointed out.

"Sonia," said Coach B. "Let's move those feet in. I know you haven't played double-A ball before. So let's work on just making contact with a basic batting stance. Once you start whacking the ball all over the place, we can talk about messing around with your stance."

"But, if I hit good with the basic stance, why should I change?"

The coach smiled. "Exactly."

Soon it was Mo's turn to hit. Coach B.'s arm appeared through the gap in the screen and the ball whizzed toward the strike zone. Mo brought his bat up to swing. But he didn't swing. The ball crossed the middle of the plate, at his knees.

"Strike one!" called the coach. "This is batting practice. Don't be *taking*!"

So Mo swung hard at the next pitch and got nothing but air. Then, another swing and a miss. And another.

Mo's dad had moved from the stands and was now standing right outside the batting cage.

"Little Mo, you've got to keep looking at the ball," said the coach. "You're pulling your head up as you swing. Keep your head down and on the ball."

"Okay, Coach."

Mo fouled off the next pitch, weakly. It dribbled just a few feet away.

"Better," said the coach. "We'll work on bringing your hips around. But that will come later. Right now, I just want to get your hands moving. I know that there is a long break between baseball seasons. It's easy to lose your timing over a long winter. You will get it back."

"Um, maybe I have the timing of a player who should not be playing in double A," Mo said.

"Ha, well that is not a choice, is it?" laughed Coach B. "I mean, we don't have an A program anymore.

Easy Out

We decided to move the program to double A. So here we are."

Yup, here we are, thought Mo.

Mo could hear a deep exhale from his dad. Almost a sigh. Then he heard him quietly say, "We've got a lot of work to do."

5 Pop-Ups and DEEP FLIES

The two Mos got out of the pickup truck. Little Mo walked up the driveway toward the front door of their house.

"Not so fast," his dad said. "Backyard. Now."

Mo's dad had already grabbed an old baseball glove that had been lying in the backseat of the truck. Inside the pocket of its glove was an old, beaten-up baseball.

Mo just nodded and followed his dad, his blue equipment bag slung over his shoulder.

Once they got around the house, Mo was ordered to get his glove out of the bag. Mo watched his dad take off his jacket, revealing a PROPERTY OF TORONTO BLUE JAYS T-shirt.

"But, Dad," Mo said. "We just had practice. It's almost dark."

"Now, Mo. I was watching you today. Your timing is off. Your throws are wide. Your glove isn't in the right position."

"But my shoulder is a bit sore."

"You can rest it tomorrow."

As soon as Mo got his glove on, his dad fired the baseball toward him. Mo got the glove up just in time to keep the ball from hitting him square on the nose. But he didn't catch it. It squirted out of the glove and rolled a few feet away.

"Pick it up," said his dad. "Throw it to me."

Mo picked the ball up and threw it.

"Dad," he said. "Last year you weren't so freaked out about how I was doing in baseball."

"That's because it was A-ball," said his dad. "That's just glorified house league. But now, well, this year, it's real rep baseball."

"What if we were just fine in A?" asked Mo.

His dad hunched over, put his hands on his knees, and laughed. "No one, I mean no one, is happy playing in A when they could be playing in double A. And maybe, down the road, even triple A."

"But maybe we were," said Mo. "It wasn't like we were killing everyone in A."

"No, you weren't. But you also didn't have to take it that seriously or push yourself. Playing against better teams will make all of you better players. Now, catch the ball."

His dad caught Mo's throw and threw the ball back to him again. And again. Each time Mo's dad brought his arm up to throw, Mo saw the deep scar on his elbow. It was as if someone had taken a piece of white chalk and drawn a line across his skin.

Pop-Ups and Deep Flies

★ ★ ★

The sun shone brightly on Keller Field on Saturday. The cold April winds had given way to the kind of spring afternoon that made kids think about summer vacation. It made farmers think about getting their seeds into the ground. It was like the world had woken up from a long sleep.

Coach B. had sent out an e-mail blast warning that he wanted parents to stay during the practice. They were to be ready for a meeting afterward.

Coach B. and his assistant, Coach Rau, were hitting lazy fly balls into the sky. The players stood in a line, waiting to show they could catch the sky-high pops.

Sonia Semeniuk wore dark blue shades to screen against the glare. The ball looked like it disappeared into the sun before heading back to Earth. Sonia put her glove up and the ball landed in it. She squeezed and the ball remained firmly in place. She didn't look anything like the unsure fielder from the first day in the school gym.

"Nice catch," called Coach B. "That's how it's done."

"First try!" Sonia nodded.

But Sonia's catch didn't set the tone for the rest of the drill. The next six players got nowhere near the ball. Each one ran around the outfield randomly and put up their gloves aimlessly. The balls dropped to the ground.

"Hey, the newbie is beating all of you guys!" Coach B. laughed.

Then it was Mo's turn. He saw Coach B. toss the ball up and smack it with the fungo bat. The ball went up, up into the sky, its red laces spinning madly. Mo began jogging to the spot where he thought the ball would land, making sure not to take his eye off the ball. Until the moment he couldn't see it anymore.

Oh, the sun! The bright afternoon sun. The ball just disappeared into the blinding light.

Mo began to shuffle as he waited for the ball to appear again. *It must be on its way down by now*, he thought. And there it was. Mo wasn't close to where it was going to land, after all. The prairie wind and the sun had transformed the pop fly into a real adventure.

The ball hit the ground with a dull thud.

"Tough sun," Coach B. called out. Coach Rau nodded.

"Hey!" Big Mo's voice called out from the stands. "I did *not* take two hours away from the store on a busy Saturday afternoon to see that kind of effort!"

Mo exhaled and closed his eyes. He tossed his glove to the ground and gave it a mighty kick.

"Hey!" came his dad's voice again. "If you want to play soccer, just let me know. Your mother can take you to all the games and practices, then."

★ ★ ★

Coaches B. and Rau stood just outside the diamond, right next to the stands where the parents and players were seated.

"Okay, I want to thank everyone for coming to our tryouts," Coach B. said. "First off, for those of you who don't know me because I haven't sold you a truck, my name is Joe Bilodeau. I have years of experience playing rep ball. When I was younger, I was on the Legionnaires team. Maybe I didn't need to tell you that. Anyhow, I've taken some courses to get certified as a coach. I'd like to quickly talk about one of those courses, Respect in Sport. One of the big things it tells you is to have realistic expectations for your kids. This is year one for the program in double A. So we're not going to win tier-one provincials. We need to be patient as these kids adjust to a new level. Heck, I have a kid who hasn't played ball at all before this year. How can a kid who has never played ball make a double-A team? As you can tell, this isn't so much a tryout as it is a training camp."

As the parents nodded, Coach B. went on. "That's just the reality of rep sports. Not everyone wants to make the commitment. So, to the twelve players and their families, your dedication is noted. It is an awfully big deal for Westlock to have a double-A team again. It's a big step up, and we're going to be going up against some very, very good teams from across Alberta."

He paused for a second, letting his words sink in.

"Now, before I tell you that our team is set with these twelve players, I want to let you all know what this will mean. There will be road trips across Alberta. We will be staying in hotels. We will need volunteers to score the games. We will need people to rake the diamond and paint the lines when we play at home. We will need someone to keep track of the pitch count, because no pitcher at this age is allowed to throw more than seventy pitches in a week. This is a big commitment for families. If you didn't know that coming in, take the next few days to think about it and let me know. I'm not going to make you decide here and now. Let us know by the end of the week. If I don't hear from anyone, I'll assume we're all good."

"Are you kidding?" Big Mo exploded. "We have all been waiting for this! Go, Westlock!"

6 OVERWHELMED

The Westlock team was gathered at the Legion Memorial Ballpark in St. Albert, Alberta. Even though spring had still not fully taken hold, the grass was bright green. The lines on the diamond were bright white. The red shale that marked the infield was raked perfectly flat.

The Westlock parents found seats in the stands behind the plate as the kids began to unload their bags in the dugout on the first-base side.

"I had heard that St. Albert has the nicest fields in Alberta," said Remi. "But seeing is believing! Look at this dugout . . . it's even got hooks for our stuff. That grass in the outfield is cut so short, it looks like a golf course. We never played on a field this nice in A-ball!"

Coach B. walked into the dugout. He had shaved off his scraggly beard. He had a steaming cup of coffee in his hand. His smile was as wide as that of a circus clown. He wore a bright blue jacket with WESTLOCK stitched in red on the front.

"Okay, kids. Quick meeting!" he said. He took a long gulp of coffee.

Mo counted eleven players sitting quietly on the dugout bench. There was a player missing. After Coach B.'s speech at the last "tryout," Mo wasn't too surprised that one of the families had left.

"All right, this is an exhibition game," Coach B. smiled. "That means it won't count in the standings. But this game still matters. This is our first chance to get out there as a team. Okay, the St. Albert Cardinals have one of the best programs in the province. They have so many kids playing ball around here that they have a first team and a second team and a third team. For all I know, they have twentieth and twenty-first teams, too. Their second team, the one we're facing today, is going to be tough. Let me tell you, their second team will be a lot better than the top double-A teams from most other programs."

"So we are facing their double-A, number-two team. Are we talking in code?" Mo asked.

This prompted a bit of laughter in the dugout. Even Coach B. cracked a smile. "Okay, good to see you are all loose. But what I need is to see you all at your best. The time for pretending is over, the time for performing is now."

Coach Rau stood just outside the dugout. His blue mirrored sunglasses reflected the bright sunlight. His lips were pencil-line thin and closed.

Overwhelmed

Put him in a suit and he would look like one of those bodyguards the prime minister has, thought Mo.

Coach B. read out the lineup. Mo was going to hit in the lead-off spot. He would be playing shortstop. Remi was put at first base, but was hitting way down in ninth spot.

"Don't worry," said the coach. "We are going to try you in different positions today. Two of you will need to sit out each inning. We will figure things out ahead of our first real game next week."

The St. Albert diamond had an announcer who sat in a shack right behind the backstop.

"Batting first for Westlock, Mo Mountpet. Sorry. Number 1, Mo Montpetit!"

As a left-handed batter, Mo stepped into the batter's box on the right side of home plate. He dug his cleats into the red dirt. The pitcher, all dressed in red, coiled up and then extended one leg toward the plate. His right arm snapped forward. The ball was a blur.

"Strike one!" the umpire called from behind the plate.

Whoa, Mo thought. *That's the fastest pitch I've ever faced.*

Mo stepped out of the batter's box to look to where his dad was sitting in the stands. His dad just shook his head.

Mo stepped back into the box. The pitcher coiled. The ball was fired toward the plate. Mo stepped forward and swung hard, hoping that the blur would come somewhere near his bat. It didn't. The pitch had been wild — nowhere near the strike zone.

Mo took a deep breath.

"Way to get the hands moving!" called Coach B. from the dugout. "Just be more selective."

Mo didn't swing at the next pitch. The ball came out of the pitcher's hand so fast, Mo had no idea if it was going to be a ball or strike.

When he heard the umpire call, "Ball one," Mo sighed in relief.

"Just throw it down the middle!" the St. Albert coach called to his pitcher. "One more, no more!"

The pitcher peered in toward his catcher. He scowled, and then reared back and threw.

This looks like it might be a strike, Mo thought. But in the split-second he should have started his swing, Mo froze. And the pitch went by.

"Strike three!"

7 The MERCY RULE

Mo wasn't the only person to strike out that first inning in the game against St. Albert. Sonia Semeniuk went down. The team's third hitter, Leon LeMay, stayed hunched over for almost a minute after a pitch hit him in the stomach. He winced as Coach Rau helped him get to first base. But the team's fourth hitter, Bobby Hu, flailed three times at three consecutive strikes, so Leon never made it past first.

The game moved to the bottom of the first inning. It was time for Mo to go to shortstop. Kaden Corbett was the starting pitcher. He threw three balls past the Westlock catcher in the warm-up.

"Hey," a St. Albert parent yelled at the lead-off batter. "I think your kid brother throws harder than this guy does!"

As it turned out, the hitter didn't need to swing. Corbett threw four straight pitches that were nowhere near the plate. The hitter walked to first. When the next hitter came up, Corbett threw a wild pitch and the base runner jogged to second. Then he went to third on the next wild pitch.

Finally, Corbett threw a pitch down the middle. The hitter took a swing but didn't get all of the ball. Instead of a nice, hard line drive, the hit was a grounder toward . . . the shortstop.

Mo crouched and got his glove down toward the dirt. Just like he had been taught in A-ball. He had the ball lined up. Before he had the ball in his glove, he began to think about his throw to first. How he'd need to get it on target.

The ball went right into Mo's glove. Mo got out of his crouch and took the ball from his glove with his throwing hand. He looked at first base, drew his arm back, and threw. The ball went so high over Remi's head the first baseman would have had to be at least ten feet tall to catch it.

The hitter wasn't only safe at first, but also got to jog to second on Mo's throwing error. The runner who was on third went home. St. Albert was up 1-0 after just two batters.

And that was just the start.

Seven batters later, St. Albert had scored six runs and had the bases loaded. Still no outs.

The next hitter took a big swing at Corbett's pitch and blasted it over the head of Sonia at centre field. The base runners took off. But when the runner from third crossed the plate, the umpire threw up his hands to call time out. Sonia hadn't even retrieved the ball.

"That's seven! Inning over!" the umpire yelled.

The Westlock players walked toward the dugout.

Coach B. clapped his hands. "Okay, let's get on the bats!"

"What just happened?" Sonia asked.

"That's right, you're new. It's the mercy rule," Remi said. "If a team scores seven runs in an inning, the inning is over."

"Oh."

"It gets worse. If we're ten runs down by the end of our at-bat in the fifth inning, or down by eight or more after the sixth, the game is ended. It's called being mercied. And we're well on our way."

Remi's prediction that Westlock would be down by ten in the fifth inning was wrong. In fact, it was 21–0 when the fifth inning began. Even if Westlock could turn things around and score the maximum seven runs in the fifth, they would still be down fourteen. So, no matter what, this was the last inning before a mercy would be declared by the umpire.

Mo was up again.

No pressure. We're going to lose, anyway, he thought.

St. Albert had brought in a new pitcher. One who didn't throw nearly as hard as the starter. But it took him just three pitches to sit Mo down. Mo's bat never left his shoulder.

Mo's dad continued to stare and shake his head.

The game ended at 21–0. St. Albert didn't even have to bat for a fifth time. With the gap at far more than ten runs in the middle of the fifth, the home-plate umpire raised his hands and called a merciful end to the game.

The Westlock players and coaches lined up at the plate so they could shake the hands of the St. Albert players. Mo noticed that many of the St. Albert players were trying not to make eye contact when they said "good game" and walked past.

Man, they are embarrassed to have beaten us this bad, Mo thought.

Then came Sonia Semeniuk's voice. "Wow. We really, really suck."

Coach Rau whispered something in Coach B.'s ear as they walked back to the dugout. Mo was close enough to hear, "Man, we have a lot of work to do."

Darn straight you do, Mo thought.

"Practice this week, Tuesday and Thursday!" Coach B. called out when he got to the dugout. "We have to be better than this next week. We're playing for real! This game ended up being cut so short, I didn't get a chance to see everyone play in the different spots that I'd hoped."

Coach Rau tapped Coach B. on the shoulder.

"Oh, what's that?" Coach B. snorted. "Oh, right! Okay, enough with the doom and gloom. I wanted to let you all know that we have snagged an invite to the big Lloydminster tournament. We have a couple of months to get ready for that, but it will feature some of the best teams in Saskatchewan and Alberta. We'll see how we measure up."

Oh, no. No. No. Mo thought. *We are so not ready. Not now. Not ever. I thought Coach B. talked about having realistic expectations. What is realistic about sending us all the way to Lloydminster to play some of the best teams in the west?*

On the way home, Mo's dad broke his silence in the pickup truck as they headed north on the highway.

"What was that? A couple of strikeouts," Big Mo said. "And, man, your team dropped more balls in one inning than we used to in a full season. I mean, does Joe need help with this team? Is he in over his head? You kids should be doing a lot better. You especially, Mo. Come on. You didn't even swing at some pitches down the middle. And let me tell you . . ."

Mo looked at the digital clock on the truck's dashboard. He was pretty sure his dad had begun his rant at 6:14. It was now 6:17.

The rant went on.

6:21: "And let me tell you, when I was your age, if I made an error like that, it just ate me alive. It would keep me up at night . . ."

And on.

6:24: "It's all a matter of focus. You can't lose focus

in the game. I know if your pitcher is walking batter after batter, it's easy to let your mind wander. But as soon as you do, I guarantee the ball will be hit out to you, so you have to be ready . . ."

A sign on the highway read *Westlock 44 km.*

Forty-four kilometres till I'm saved, Mo thought.

8 The Season BEGINS

The pickup truck pulled into the parking lot. A number of baseball diamonds were spread throughout Callingwood Park in West Edmonton. Mo wondered why the team they were playing was called the South Jasper Park Jays. After all, wasn't this an Edmonton team?

Remi was in the truck with Mo and his dad.

"Are we ready for this?" Mo asked.

"Sure are," his dad said from behind the wheel. But Mo could tell from his dad's voice that he wasn't sure at all.

"I don't think we're ready," said Remi. "I mean, we might as well play, because I don't know if all the practice in the world will make us any better. But I guess if we do better than 21–0, we're on the way up."

"Let's do better than losing by twenty-one!" Mo raised his hand in the air and laughed. His laugh stopped short when he caught his dad's icy stare.

Mo thought back to the practices earlier in the week. Leon LeMay had earned the nickname "Ball Magnet."

He had been rushed to the Westlock Healthcare Centre after a batting-practice pitch had struck him square in the face. There had been dropped fly balls. There had been ground balls that had gone through legs. And the ball could have been the size of a pea when he recalled the number of times the Westlock players had swung and missed during batting practice.

Cars trickled into the parking lot, and the skies hung gloomy over the field. The boys changed into their white jerseys. South Jasper had dark blue shirts on.

"They played earlier today," Coach B. told his players as they lined up for the pre-game batting practice. "As you guys might know, there will be days in the schedule where teams play more than one game. And I was told that South Jasper burned their ace pitcher in their earlier game. He has reached his limit of seventy pitches for the weekend. So let's go out there and take some hacks on whoever they send up against us."

Coach B. and Coach Rau each carried a bucket of soft orange balls into the grass outfield. The players grabbed helmets and bats. Bobby Hu and Mark Laboucaine went first, because the starting pitcher and catcher always hit first in pre-game batting practice. That way they could leave first, to focus on warming up in the bullpen.

Both Bobby and Mark rapped some balls smartly that landed near the outfield fence. The coaches tossed balls softly. With each successful swing, the orange soft ball made a *thud* as it was launched off the bat.

"So far, not bad," Mo whispered to Remi.

When Mo got to bat, he made contact with his first swing. All right! The ball barely got back to Coach B., but at least he had hit it. That was a start.

"Okay, Mo, now put a little more of your hips into the swing," Coach B. nodded. "Now drive the ball. Explosive hips!"

Mo fouled off the next two pitches, then hit a couple of harmless grounders out toward his coach.

"Hey, you can beat those out," the coach said. "Sometimes, those dribblers work out just fine. Just hustle up the first-base line and they might not be able to beat you with the throw."

Meanwhile, Remi was being pitched to by Coach Rau. He took five big swings. His cheeks puffed out as he brought the bat through the strike zone. But each time he got nothing but air.

"Come on, Remi," Coach Rau said, his voice flat. "Don't take your eye off the ball. Keep your head on the ball. Don't look up or away from the ball as you swing."

"Yes, Coach," Remi smiled.

"At least you're not *tomahawking* the ball," Mo snickered.

With a cheeky smile, Remi raised his middle finger toward his best friend.

As the on-field warm-ups drew to a close, some

Westlock players pointed excitedly toward South Jasper's bullpen. Mo looked beside the dugout on the third-base side of the diamond.

"Look, the pitcher has a ponytail," Leon pointed. "Holy . . . their pitcher is a girl!"

"Come on," said Mark. "Oh, come on. I can't believe they are going to start a girl against us. We're going to be okay. We're going to get some hits!"

"Guys, I'm right here," Sonia barked as she put her hands on her head.

"Sorry, Sonia," said Mark. "But, I mean, we all know there's no way she's going to throw as hard as any of the boys."

"Go on," Sonia said coldly.

"Look, I'm just saying we have to take advantage of this. We're going to score some runs!"

Sonia pulled her cap down so it covered most of her face. "Save me," she said, her voice muffled.

South Jasper's pitcher and catcher walked out of the bullpen and onto the diamond as their teammates took the field.

"Just a few last warm-up pitches," the umpire cried as the pitcher got to the mound.

"Okay, everyone, pay attention!" said Coach B. "Watch the warm-ups. Time the pitcher!"

She toed the rubber, took a big stride and *whack*! It was the sound of the ball hitting the leather of the catcher's mitt.

Whack!

Whack! Whack!

Mo had never seen any pitcher throw that hard outside of the games he watched on TV. She threw way harder than the St. Albert pitcher.

"So she's *not* their best pitcher?" Mo asked. He took a big gulp.

"That's what they said," Remi said. "We are in so much trouble, aren't we?"

Coach B. snorted. "Come on guys, you can get a hit off her."

"Realistic expectations," Mo said under his breath.

9 Sliding INTO HOME

Coach B. taped the team's lineup to the dugout wall.

"Why am I hitting lead-off and starting the game at shortstop?" Mo whispered to Remi.

Remi just jerked his thumb in the direction of the stands behind home plate where Mo's father sat.

"You're royalty, don't you know?" Remi whispered. He followed it up with a bow and then put on the worst English accent Mo had ever heard. "Honoured to be standing next to you, my Lord."

Mo rolled his eyes, then grabbed his black batting helmet and the lighter of the two bats from his equipment bag. *She brings it, so I'll need to get the bat moving quickly*, thought Mo. He walked out of the dugout toward the on-deck circle. He slid the hitting weight onto the bat and took a couple of mighty swings.

The umpire called, "Play ball!"

Mo banged his bat on the ground to loosen the weight and slide it off. He strolled into the batter's box on the first-base side of the plate.

"Strike one!" the umpire called as the first pitch whizzed by Mo. The South Jasper infielders cheered.

Then came the next pitch. Mo saw the white blur rocket toward him.

Wait, that's toward me. Not the plate.

Mo took a quick step back and ducked, turning his face away from the pitch. The ball made a dull thud as it hit him in the shoulder. He winced, fighting back tears that came to his eyes. It stung, but he gritted his teeth.

Coach Rau walked toward Mo from the coaching box behind first base.

"You okay?" came the flat voice.

Mo squinted hard and nodded. He ground his teeth together.

"Look! He's crying!" called a kid from the infield. "I thought crying was done back when we were playing T-ball!"

I am not crying, thought Mo. He wanted to check that his cheeks were dry, but that would look like he was wiping away tears.

Coach Rau took Mo by the arm and escorted him to first base. "He'll be fine," he told the ump.

The players on the Westlock bench clapped.

"Our first baserunner of the game!" Mo heard his dad's voice from the stands. "Way to go, Mo!"

Remi was next at bat. He fouled off a couple of pitches. Then he took a huge swing at a ball that bounced as it got to the plate.

The catcher blocked it. Remi started to run, but the umpire stopped him. "At this level, you can't run on a dropped third strike," he told Remi.

So Remi turned around and walked back to the dugout.

Leon LeMay came up and stuck his bat out. It made contact with the ball, which bounced directly to the pitcher. Mo took off and went to second. He heard the umpire call LeMay out at first after the pitcher made a perfect throw to her teammate.

That left Saad Almasi. The first pitch to him was wide of the catcher and went all the way to the backstop. Mo ran as fast as he could toward third base. He took a mighty slide that skinned his knee, even though the third baseman was calling for the catcher to "eat it" and not bother throwing the ball.

On the next two pitches, Saad was nowhere near the ball with his swings. Coach B., who was in the third-base-side coaching box, leaned over and whispered to Mo, "We're having a hard time catching up to her pitches. If a pitch gets away from the catcher, even just a little bit, take off for the plate."

Mo nodded.

Maybe Coach B. could tell the future. The next pitch skipped before it got to the plate, and bounced off the catcher's shin guard.

"Go!" Coach B. yelled.

"He's going!" the third baseman called.

Mo ran toward home plate as fast as he could. The catcher scrambled to find the ball. It was slowly rolling away from him, toward the backstop. He found the ball, picked it up and fired it toward the pitcher. She had run to the plate to take the throw.

Mo slid, even though his knee burned from his slide into third. The pitcher got her glove down to make the tag. Too late! The umpire swung his hands back and forth.

"SAFE!"

A giant cheer went up from the Westlock bench.

★ ★ ★

It didn't last. In the bottom of the first, Bobby walked the first three South Jasper batters he faced. Then a ground ball went right through the legs of Kaden Corbett at first base and slowly rolled down the right-field line. All of the runners, including the batter, scored. Westlock didn't register an out before South Jasper scored seven.

And then seven in the next inning.

In the third inning, a ground ball was hit toward Mo at shortstop. Even though the ball took a bit of an awkward bounce where the dirt met the infield grass, Mo was able to track it down.

And then Mo felt his heart rate rise. Kaden stood at first base, glove ready. But it was like Mo had forgotten everything he'd worked on in practice. He didn't set his feet. He didn't rotate through his hips. All he could think about was his dad watching him. And the ball sailed over Kaden's head. The runner rounded first and headed for second on the error.

To make the game even worse for Mo, he struck out on three pitches in his next at-bat.

Eventually, the umpire cried, "Mercy!"

The teams shook hands, with South Jasper up 19–1. Mo overheard the South Jasper coach and Coach B. talking in the lineup.

"Yeah, it's a struggle," said Coach B. "You guys have real tryouts and cuts. We had barely enough kids try out to put a team together. There are kids here who don't deserve to be here. They're not at double-A level. They need to learn basics like how to properly make a throw or hold the bat. But we're not in a house league, where those skills are taught. They're trying to learn how to swing while facing some of the best pitchers they could possibly see. Hey, wait, stop listening in, Mo!"

10 What's Wrong WITH WESTLOCK?

"That was terrible," Mo's dad said from behind the wheel of the pickup truck.

"You don't need to tell me that," said Mo.

"I mean, even a few weeks ago, I thought you were *good*. It seemed like some of your teammates had potential, too," said Mo's dad. "But, wow. I mean, Wow. Capital W. I don't think your team would even be a good A-ball team."

"Dad, this is our first year. And it's not like we had a real tryout. Everyone made the team. We have players on our team who have never played before. Till now, I mean."

"I know!" his dad grunted. "There was a time when fifty kids would be trying out. Competing to make the team. What's wrong with our town? Westlock *is* baseball!"

"*Was*," said Remi from the backseat.

"What?"

"Maybe baseball *was* Westlock," Remi said sadly. "It doesn't feel like it's that important to the town anymore."

Mo's father winced. "No, no. You kids will figure it out. You just need more practice time. A lot of practice time."

"Dad," said Mo. "I don't know if practice time is going to help. At least, it's not going to help someone who hasn't played at a high level all of a sudden hit fastballs from rep pitchers."

"Not true. You just have to work at it!"

"Dad," Mo took a deep breath. "If you feel so strongly about it, how come you're not our coach? How come you didn't volunteer to help Coach B.?"

"Son, the store is so busy . . ."

"Yet you always seem to make time to watch me play and take me to practice. I mean, you could take that same time and help coach the team. You know more about baseball than anyone else in town."

"Drop this, son."

Mo looked at the scar on his dad's elbow. The line disappeared under the sleeve of his T-shirt. "How come you never came back? All I heard about was how good you were. I heard there were even scouts from the U.S. looking to bring you to some big college down there."

"There were scouts, you know that. But they don't want a guy whose arm had to be rebuilt."

"You had a chance to really make it, Dad. And it didn't happen. Now all we do is talk about the past. But you have to realize I am not you. I am not your failed dream."

Mo's dad hit the brakes and jerked the steering wheel. The truck pulled over to the shoulder of the highway.

"How. Dare. You." he sneered. "*Maurice*, if you want to quit, go ahead and quit! You're just embarrassing me, anyway. Maybe this whole team was a mistake!"

His dad's words hurt Mo more than getting hit by the pitch. If they were in town, he would have opened the truck door and hopped out. He would have walked home. But they were on the highway, a long way from Westlock.

Not a word came from the back seat, where Remi sat, afraid to move a muscle.

★ ★ ★

The next day, Mo got home from school and changed into his baseball gear.

"Where's your father?" his mom asked.

"I don't think he's taking me to practice today." Mo pulled on his Property of Westlock Baseball practice shirt. "I'll get to practice myself. I think he has a lot to do today at the store."

"Now, don't tell me your dad is busy at the store," she said. "He's been getting out to every practice and game that he can. I saw you two eyeing each other at the breakfast table this morning. You must have had a fight."

Mo looked down at his feet. "Mom, I just can't do it. I can't play at this level. Heck, none of us can. We're just not good. But Coach keeps putting me at shortstop and having me hit at the top of the order, just because of who my dad is. It's not fair."

"No, it's not," said his mom. "But we can't change things, can we? I mean, unless you want me to take you to the courthouse so we can legally change your name. The problem is, you don't know this, but you look a lot like your dad did when he was younger."

"And it doesn't help that you gave me his entire name, too. The last name is bad enough."

Mo's mom crossed her arms and then uncrossed them. "Young man, come with me." She spun around and opened the door that led to the basement.

Mo followed his mom down the creaky stairs. On a shelf next to the washer and dryer stood his dad's old baseball trophies. Tournament Most Valuable Player. Team MVP. Provincial all-star. First place here, first place there. On another shelf was a box stuffed with what looked like enough medals for an entire Olympics.

"Mom, I know, I know," Mo said. "This is dad's trophy room. I'm not supposed to touch any of this stuff."

His mom didn't say a word. Near the shelves was a large cardboard box with *JUNK* scrawled on it in marker.

"Come here, Mo," his mom said as she opened the box.

What's Wrong with Westlock?

Inside were photos of a boy playing ball. *Is that me?* thought Mo. Looking closer, he saw that it was his dad. *Whoa, it's like looking in a mirror.*

There were papers in there, letters from big American universities. And, wait, was that a letter from a Major League Baseball scout? *There's no way a big-league team scouted in Westlock*, thought Mo.

His mom found a folded-up newspaper clipping and handed the yellowed piece of paper to her son. "This was the day everything changed," she said. "I know you sort of know the story. But I don't think you understand what a big deal to Westlock the accident was. Your dad wasn't just good. He was a hero to the whole town."

Westlock News

BASEBALL STAR RUSHED TO HOSPITAL

Just two months after winning the provincial championship with the Westlock Legionnaires, star infielder and pitcher Maurice Montpetit faces a long road to recovery.

Alberta Health and Safety is looking into an accident at the Westlock Independent Grocers.

"There was an incident and a worker suffered injuries," said Alberta Health and Safety spokesperson Jim Inglis. "The investigation is ongoing. We will not be discussing this case further until the process is concluded."

Montpetit has been transferred to the University of Alberta Hospital in Edmonton, where he is listed in serious condition.

His family has confirmed that he has undergone surgery on his right arm.

"Mo will be okay," said his father, Dominic Montpetit. "But he is feeling shaken right now. We're not sure how it happened, but a large number of boxes fell on him as he was taking a delivery at the store. We're worried that the damage to his arm is severe. We will know more in the coming days. We'd like to thank everyone in Westlock for respecting our privacy."

Named the top player for the Legionnaires, Montpetit won the Most Valuable Player award at the provincial championships. He was shortlisted by Baseball Canada as a "Prospect to Watch" and there has been interest from some American universities.

"He is arguably the best baseball prospect to come from Alberta," said Bill Dorne, a Canadian scout. "I mean, he's awfully young, awfully raw. So there are still a lot of unknowns there. But, this is a player who could have garnered interest from the States. Major League Baseball? Too early to tell. The NCAA? For sure."

But that career is now in doubt.

"No matter what happens, this town will look after Mo," said Ziggy Meier, owner of Westlock Independent Grocers. "He has worked for us since he was a kid. We're waiting to find out what happened, but it's a darn shame."

11 Time TO QUIT

After a drill in which Westlock team members managed to drop eight fly balls in a row, the coach told the players to put down their gloves. He had them start running on the outfield grass, from foul pole to foul pole. The players went back and forth. Mo's legs burned.

"Okay, last lap!" Coach B. bellowed. He placed two pylons in the middle of the outfield. "The last one to get from the right-field foul pole to between these two pylons has to pick up all the bases and put them away!"

The pack tried to chase Remi and Mo down, but the two friends gained a lead and held it. Leon LeMay grunted and collapsed — the last player to come through the pylons.

"Okay, practice is over!" yelled Coach B. "You guys have got to work to get better. Not just at practice, but on your own time, as well. We can't just be dropping balls like that!"

As the players went their separate ways, Mo remained behind. He shooed Remi away to make sure he would be alone with the coaches.

"Coach B.? Coach Rau?" he said.

"What is it, Little Mo?" asked Coach B.

"I'd like to make a request, sir."

"Well," Coach B. smiled. "You're already our lead-off hitter, I don't know what else you'd want."

"Actually, sir, I'm thinking about quitting the team. I mean, I think I might be embarrassing myself. At least that's what I've been told."

"What?" Coach B. hissed. Coach Rau took off his shades. Mo was pretty sure it was the first time he'd actually seen the assistant coach's eyes all season.

"Hey, now. Who said that about you? A teammate? We're all supposed to be supporting each other."

"I would rather not say. But that person is right. I think I am wasting everyone's time. I'm taking up a spot on this team and I'm not very good."

"Wait a second," Coach B. put his hands on Mo's shoulder. "Did you see that race? You finished ahead of the pack. You've got quick feet, and that's why you hit first. You've got the only run this team has scored so far this year."

"That was a fluke."

"Look, Mo, I know you're not stupid. Our program is just starting out. You're right, a lot of you kids aren't ready for double-A ball. That's for sure. You're struggling out there. And, honestly, I'm not expecting you guys to go out and win a bunch of games. This is all too much, too fast. But that's how life goes. Sometimes you're thrown in at the deep end."

"But I don't like the deep end."

"Nobody does. Look, we already lost one player. His parents pulled him out once they saw what kind of crazy schedule a double-A team has. If we go down to ten players, we'll have just one extra. If players get hurt or need to take the weekend off, we're hooped. At eleven players, I'm barely keeping the program running. If we're down to ten players, I might have to end things. I don't have anyone else stepping up."

So that's it, Mo thought. *If I quit, the team might end.*

"I guess I have to stay, then," he said.

"If the kid wants to quit, we should let him quit." Coach Rau's voice broke in. "If he doesn't want to be here, why should we force him to play? If he doesn't want to quit, we should kick him off the team."

What? Mo thought. *Wait, leaving the team is my choice. I want to quit the team. I'm not getting kicked off the team.*

"I don't want you to kick me off," said Mo. "I don't want the team to fold. But I don't want to be embarrassing."

"Then try a better attitude," said Coach Rau.

"And maybe we need a better attitude, too." Coach B. turned to Coach Rau. "Let's go back to our coaching courses. We need to set realistic goals for this kid. For all the kids. We need to work on catching balls and making contact rather than winning games. We need to set more reachable goals for the team. If a Montpetit wants to quit baseball, we must be doing something wrong."

"I know you talk about realistic goals," said Mo. "But then the games come around and all I feel is pressure. I think the rest of the team does, too."

Coach B. put up his hand, signalling to Coach Rau he didn't want to hear any more from him.

"Okay, Little Mo," said Coach B. "You stay on, and we'll work on being better coaches. Okay?"

12 The Boys Are BACK IN TOWN

The home opener was in a couple of days — and that meant the twenty-fifth anniversary was coming, too. That meant the whole town and more coming out to watch them play.

The previous night, Mo's dad had gone out after work to meet up with some of the guys who had come back to town to be part of the celebration. One was an executive with some oil company in Calgary. There was one who sold insurance in Saskatoon. Another guy ran a feedlot in a town smaller than Westlock. And there was one guy who had moved to the United States. How Mo even remembered any of these details was beyond him.

The more his dad talked about the big anniversary, the more Mo looked at the weather app he'd just installed on his phone. It showed that there was a 50 per cent chance of thunderstorms for Saturday. Mo had gone online and checked the Baseball Alberta handbook. If there was lightning, they couldn't play.

Of course, whoever scheduled the games had made

sure their opponents were going to be the Barrhead Orioles.

"When we get mercied by Barrhead, my dad will disown me," Mo said to Remi during a break between classes.

"Well, maybe everyone will be way too far into their trip down memory lane to notice," said Remi. "You know what my dad told me? Twenty-five years ago, after they won the provincial title, that Westlock team got a parade. Like a pro team would if they won the World Series!"

"Oh, I know," said Mo. "My dad has mentioned the parade only about once a day, for every day I've been alive."

★ ★ ★

Mo rolled out of bed, rubbed his eyes and walked zombie-like to the bathroom. He was halfway through brushing his teeth when he remembered it was Saturday morning. Game day. Anniversary day.

"Hustle up, Mo!" he heard his dad call from the living room. "Some of the boys are coming over and we're all going to head to the park together!"

Mo finished brushing his teeth, then dashed back to his bedroom, where his phone was sitting on his dresser. He opened the weather app and hoped. There it was:

TODAY: 60% chance of rain, possible severe thunderstorms in the early afternoon.

Possible, Mo thought. *Possible.*

It was too early to change into his uniform, so he put on a T-shirt and shorts and headed downstairs.

What the heck?

His dad was in the living room. He wore the blue cap with the red W. And a shiny blue jacket that was oh-so-very tight. On it was *Westlock* in red script. And then, bright white baseball pants, with a bright blue belt.

"Um, dad?"

"Ha! We all talked about it, and we're going to the anniversary in uniform!" His dad was beaming. "Barry at the sports store made replicas for all of us, too bad they are all the same size! I don't know how some of us are going to fit into these things, but we'll do our best!"

"Wow, Dad. You are so, so, so . . . shiny," said Mo.

"Isn't he?" His mom walked in with a coffee mug in her hand just as the doorbell rang.

"One of the boys must be a bit early!" said his dad. Mo followed him to the door.

Mo's dad opened the door, and it was as if his clone was standing there. The man had the same cap, the same shimmering blue jacket, the same awful white baseball pants.

"Ricky-Robb!" his dad cried, and the two men

hugged. Mo tried to remember the last time his dad had hugged *him* like that.

"This must be Mo," said Ricky-Robb, extending his hand. "My name is Rick. The last name is Robb. With two Bs. So everyone calls me Ricky-Robb."

That sounds like a made-up name, thought Mo. *Like a name a pro wrestler would have. Or a name from a book where the writer can only think of goofy names to give people.*

"So, this is the young baseball star," said Ricky-Robb, as he punched Mo in the shoulder. "Your dad says you're pretty good. But you'd have to be really good, I mean super-awesome, to be better than your dad was . . ."

A flash. Mo began to ignore Ricky-Robb's conversation at the moment he saw it. Could it be? Out the window? Wait. There it was again. Lightning in the distance! And it looked like the clouds were rolling in toward town!

". . . and, well, kid, you should get in that uniform right away. We don't want to be late for that game against Barrhead. I mean, you probably didn't sleep at all knowing that you've got Barrhead coming to town!"

"Yes, sir," Mo nodded, pretending he was listening. "But . . . um, and this sucks, but it looks like a bad storm might be blowing in. I mean, it would be awful if we had to postpone. Because, yeah, we've all been looking forward to this big home opener."

The Boys Are Back in Town

Big Mo and Ricky-Robb looked out the window just in time to see forked lightning lash the prairie. Their backs were turned to Mo, so he allowed himself a bit of a smile.

★ ★ ★

The rain sheeted down as people ran from their cars in the parking lot to the doors of the community centre next to Keller Field.

There were waterlogged paper signs taped to the doors.

BARRHEAD vs. WESTLOCK U13 RAINED OUT. LEGIONNAIRES 25th ANNIVERSARY MOVED INDOORS. COME INSIDE!

"They're still going through with this stupid thing," Mo whispered to Remi as they each got a bag of chips from the concession stand. "At least the game is off, though."

"Look at this place." Remi waved his arm. "Packed. There must be a few hundred people in here. I mean, not a seat in the place. I see Mama Wilson out there in the corner. And no one has seen her leave her house in two years!"

"I just assumed she was dead," said Mo.

"Well, the twenty-fifth anniversary of the Best Day Ever has brought her back to life."

A woman walked up to the microphone. She

introduced herself as the editor of the local newspaper. A couple of people responded with light-hearted boos.

"I'm your host for the day. I know this isn't the way we planned to do it," she said. "But Mother Nature rained on our parade . . ." She paused, waiting for the laughter from the crowd. There was none. "Okay, I know how important winning the provincial title was to this town twenty-five years ago. I looked through some old newspaper clippings and I was amazed. Really! Beating teams from Edmonton and Red Deer and Calgary and points in between. Incredible."

"And Barrhead!" roared Big Mo. "We kicked Barrhead's butt!"

That earned a roar from the crowd.

A dozen men sat in a row next to the host, all in too-tight blue team jackets. One of them wasn't able to button his up.

The host spoke again. "Well, we're here to welcome them all. Please, Westlock, stand up and give a big hand to your older and greyer Westlock Legionnaires!"

The people stood and whooped and hollered. The twenty-fifth anniversary team members stood up, took off their caps and waved them. Mo caught his mom's gaze. She was standing in the row closest to the host. She gave Mo a thumbs-up.

"This whole town lives in the past," Remi shouted into Mo's ear.

"And my parents are leading them there," said Mo.

13 Play of the SEASON

It didn't rain the following weekend. And that was bad news for the Westlock AA team. The Whitecourt Royals came to Keller Field and scored seven runs in the top of the first.

"We actually got two outs before they got to seven!" Kaden Corbett said as the Westlock players ran into the dugout.

There were a few groans, but Mo cut in. "You know what? He's right. Look, everyone. This is an improvement."

"We all know we're getting our butts kicked again," said Kaden. "But maybe not as hard this time. I just wanted to point out that we *almost* got out of the inning."

The Whitecourt pitcher took to the mound and began his warm-up. The Westlock team watched as the ball didn't exactly zip into the catcher's mitt.

"Wait, this guy doesn't throw very hard!" Sonia Semeniuk clapped her hands.

"Good news," said Coach B. "It looks like they burned their best pitcher in their game on Friday night.

So I think their best arm is gone."

"Or they've looked at our stats," Mo said as he put on his batting helmet. "They know they don't need to waste their best pitcher against us."

"Hey!" Coach B. snapped. Everyone on the bench froze. "I understand things haven't gone our way yet this season. But it's no reason for anyone on this team to get down on themselves or their teammates. So shape up, Mo! I know you might think your last name gives you a free pass. Just remember, I can bat you last and stick you out in right field!"

"Promise?" Mo asked under his breath. He walked to the on-deck circle and took a couple of practice swings. And then, a little louder. "So much for taking the pressure off, Coach."

"Balls in!" the umpire cried. "Batter!"

Mo strolled into the batter's box.

"Come on, kid!" he heard his dad call from the stands.

The pitcher took a big kick and threw. The ball didn't come toward the plate all that fast. It reminded Mo of how pitchers threw in A-ball.

"Ball one!" cried the ump.

The pitch had crossed the plate, but at eye-height. The catcher tossed the ball back to the pitcher. Mo waited for the second pitch.

Mo took a hard swing, and made contact. *Crack!* The ball soared past the infield, but it was hooking toward the right-field foul line.

Stay fair! Mo thought.

"Stay fair!" Big Mo cried.

But it didn't. The ball came down a few feet on the wrong side of the foul line.

"Good swing!" Coach B. called from third-base coaching box. "That's it, Montpetit!"

The next pitch bounced before it hit the plate. Mo didn't swing.

"Ball two!"

Mo felt it in his bones. He knew the next pitch would be a strike. And then it came out of the pitcher's hand. The ball looked like a balloon, big and hardly moving. Mo shifted his weight to his back foot, then started turning his body hard through the hips. The hands followed, the bat whipping through the strike zone. It was perfect.

Crack!

This time, the ball wasn't going foul. It flew deep to centre field. Mo put his head down and ran. He rounded first and slid hard into second.

But why were all the Whitecourt players cheering? Why was the umpire standing near second base calling him out?

Mo looked back toward centre field in horror. Standing there was the Whitecourt centre fielder, holding the ball in his glove.

"What a catch! Our play of the season!" cried the Whitecourt coach.

14 Too Much PRESSURE

Mo followed his dad into the living room. His dad motioned for him to sit down. Mo sat down.

"So, 18–1," his dad said.

"We scored a run," said Mo.

"Yup, that Kaden kid hit a home run. A run to make it 12–1. And your bench celebrated like you guys won the World Series."

"It was our best hit of the year, Dad."

"Who cares?" Mo's dad growled. "You guys are embarrassing this town every time you go out there! This town has a tradition!"

Mo balled up his fists. "Hey, my first at-bat I hit the ball well."

"You did, I'll give you that. But they still found a way to turn it into an out. Because they catch the ball. Not like you guys. How many ground balls went through your legs today?"

"Two," Mo replied.

"And the one wild throw that was nowhere near

first base," his dad reminded him.

"Well, if it had been near first base, it wouldn't have been a wild throw." *Why did I just do that?* Mo thought. *Do I want Dad to explode?*

"You like being cheeky, son," his dad said. "You think it makes up for the fact that you and your teammates just don't seem to want to get any better."

"You don't see it, Dad, because we're losing as bad as we are. But we *are* getting better. We're hitting some balls and making some plays."

"Just not *most* of the plays."

"Look, I'm sorry that we're not the Legionnaires!" Mo exploded. It was like a bomb had gone off deep in his gut and was pushing everything out. "I'm sorry we're not going to win the provincial championship! I'm sorry we're not going to get a parade. And, Dad, I am sorry for not being you!"

His dad's face went red.

Mo couldn't stop now. "I'm sorry that I'm not as good as you. And I'm sorry that you had that accident. I'm sorry you didn't get that shot to play ball in the States. I'm sorry that, every day, you want me to make up for all the bad things that happened to you!"

His dad put his face in his hands.

Mo exhaled deeply. His mother walked into the room. "Maurice Montpetit! You apologize to your father this instant! That tone of voice is not acceptable."

Mo's dad spoke weakly. His voice was muffled

because his hands were still over his face. "No, Monica. It's okay. He's right."

Then he turned back to Mo. "I am so sorry," he said softly.

"What?" said Mo. "Dad?"

Mo had never seen his dad cry before. *Should I hug him? Leave him be?* Seeing his dad cry just felt wrong. Like a June snowstorm. Or like Leon LeMay saying his two favourite teams were the Yankees *and* the Red Sox.

"I know you talked to Joe B. about quitting the team," Mo's dad said. "He told me. And I've just been so mad. Like 'how dare you hate baseball?' And then . . ."

"Dad, I don't hate baseball. I like baseball," Mo said.

"I know. I see that. But what you hate is *me*."

"I don't hate you, Dad. But sometimes it feels like having the same name as you is like a weight around my ankles. You are a legend in this town."

"Son, you didn't ever see your dad play," his mom interrupted. "He was special. But he never slacked off. He wanted to get into a U.S. school on a baseball scholarship so much."

"But no one wants to take a chance on a guy who gets his throwing arm crushed by crates filled with tomato soup," said Mo's dad. "And last year, when I saw you playing A-ball with your friends . . . Well, it got Coach B. and me talking about starting up the double-A program. I wanted you to have the same chances I did."

"Wait," Mo said. "Are you saying the double-A program was started because I began playing with the single-A team?"

"Well, not exactly," his dad said.

"Yes," his mom sighed. "Yes it was. Your dad is paying for it, too."

"Well, the store is, through a silent sponsorship," his dad said. "But it's all a big mistake, isn't it? Instead of giving you the chance to play, I'm trying to live through you."

"Well, sort of," Mo said.

"When he says 'sort of,' it really means that he agrees with you,'" said his mom to his dad.

"Dad, if this means so much to you, why aren't you helping coach the team?" Mo asked. "How come you don't even play for a community slo-pitch team?"

His dad wiped a tear from his eye. "Maybe because I loved it so much. And when it all went away, I couldn't handle it. The feeling of a bat in the hand. Of the way the glove pops when you make a catch." And then his dad smiled. "And slo-pitch? Slo-pitch is *not* baseball. Slo-pitch is the worst thing in the world."

His dad laughed. And Mo laughed.

"Look," his dad said. "I put on the uniform again, we had this big anniversary to-do, and the whole town went nuts. I saw everyone standing in that arena, cheering like it was the 1990s all over again. That is, everyone was cheering except you. I looked and looked for you in that arena. And when I finally saw you, you looked about as bored as you do when you're doing math homework. And that's when I realized that I couldn't force you to care. But that's what I was trying to do before, wasn't I? I so badly wanted you to succeed at something that was taken away from me. I didn't care if you actually wanted that thing or not."

"Look, Dad," said Mo. "It's not about me wanting it or not. It's about wanting to play baseball for *me*. Not for anyone else. And no, I'm not nearly as good as you were. I do want to love baseball, but I need your help. I need you to help me, not judge me."

Mo's dad allowed himself a smile. "But what can I do? To be fair — and I'm just trying to be honest — your team is worse than bad."

"Okay, then," Mo said. "We're still a ways out from this big Lloydminster tournament. I'd like to get better. Dad, you can't live through me, but you can teach me."

Mo's dad nodded. "Look, we need to start at the beginning. Go over the basics." He paused. "Maybe I can try to help, but I'm not a miracle worker, either."

15 Back to BASICS

Keller Field was deserted except for Mo and his dad. His dad wore a twenty-five-year-old glove with a faded name tag. It was basic brown, not black or red or white or blue like the flashy new gloves. Mo carried his equipment bag.

The sun was high in the sky as the pair walked toward the batting cage. Mo's dad opened the padlock and swung open the gate. He walked inside the batting cage and Mo followed. There was a bucket of baseballs sitting in the cage behind the pitching screen. Mo took his black batting helmet out of his bag and put it on. He grabbed his bat and strode toward the plate.

His dad was behind the screen, gathering a few baseballs into his glove. "Okay, ready?" he asked.

"Sure," Mo said.

"You're not tired? This is the third day in a row that we have been doing this."

"Not tired."

"Okay."

His dad's right hand flashed forward through the gap in the screen. The ball spun toward the plate.

Mo transferred his weight from his back leg back through his hips, and then brought the bat forward. The force of the ball almost knocked the bat out of his hands. The bat rattled, and Mo felt the quiver right in his bones. It was something he had heard the baseball commentators call "bees in the hands." Now he understood what that meant.

"Good, but your swing was a little late," his dad said calmly. "You're loading up good and all. But your hands aren't coming through quick enough. I think you're pausing a bit before you commit to the swing. When you face a fast pitch, that little pause can make the difference between a base hit and a bad swing and miss. You can't have wasted movement in a baseball swing."

Mo tried to keep that all in his mind as the next pitch came toward him. *No wasted movement.*

Swing and a miss.

Another swing and a miss.

And another.

Mo waited for his dad to get angry. But all he did was grab a few more baseballs from the bucket.

"Okay, before I throw again, I know I am telling you a lot," said his dad. "Remember that hitting a baseball is the toughest thing to do in sports. It's what I read in an article once. The sweet spot is about the size of a dime. That's it. So don't worry about not being perfect. Heck, a .300 hitter makes the Hall of Fame. Hitting .300 means getting a base hit less than one out of every three tries. I think this is the greatest game in the world, but it's also the strangest. It's a sport where you're still pretty darn good even if you fail more than you succeed."

Mo smiled. He liked seeing his dad this way. The next pitch came and . . . *whack!* The bat connected crisply and the ball shot forward. It would have hit his dad square in the face if the protective screen had not been there.

"Better!" His dad smiled. "That's because you smiled. You relaxed a bit. And when you're more relaxed, you're quicker. If you're all nervous, you're tight and you get it all wrong. Relax, and your hips rotate, your hands move and you drive through the ball."

"I am not sure we're going to get this right," said Mo.

His dad threw another ball. Mo swung and missed.

"Okay, stop thinking," his dad said. "You got the one swing down, then you stopped and started worrying, so you swung and missed. Another goofy thing about baseball is that you have to do all of these little things, load through the legs, rotate the hips, keep your eyes on the ball, move your hands. But you have to clear your mind at the same time. If you think too much, it all falls apart."

Mo just nodded. *Dad's not yelling. And he's making a lot of sense about baseball. What is up?*

Another pitch came in and Mo fouled it back. Then another that he grounded wide of the pitcher's screen. Then one that — *crack!* — came flying off the bat and grazed the top of the cage.

"See? You'll get this!"

16 Three OUTS

By the time Mo got to Keller Field, the other team's players were getting out of a mini-van. On it was the logo of a tomahawk and the words *BRAVES BASEBALL.*

Remi was sitting in the dugout, waiting for his Westlock teammates to arrive.

"It's, like, well into the twenty-first century," Remi said. "And there's still a team with a tomahawk logo playing in our league."

"And that's a big deal, because . . . ?" Mo asked.

"Sometimes, Mo, you're the bestest best friend in the world," said Remi. "And sometimes I feel like you don't even know me."

Mo looked at where Mr. and Mrs. Richard were seated in the stands next to his own mom and dad.

"If you're looking at my mom to see if she has a reaction to it, don't worry about it," said Remi. "You won't see any. The thing you don't understand is the kind of stuff that's racist, but you don't even realize might be racist. We've learned to put on a straight face and just get on with it. But it doesn't mean it's right."

"Wow, this really bugs you," said Mo.

"Notice that I have a cap for every team in the league except for a select few?" asked Remi. "Think about it. Why don't I have an Indians cap? Or a Braves cap?"

Coach B. juggled the lineup. He moved Mo down to sixth in the batting order. Coach told Mo he wanted to take the pressure off him.

The Westlock team took the field in the top of the first. Leon LeMay threw a strike with his first pitch. Then the second was hit toward the centre fielder, Marquis Lee. Marquis circled below the ball, like a vulture in reverse. The ball hit his glove — and didn't come out.

First out!

"All right!" Mo yelled from where he stood, at shortstop.

But the next two hitters for the Braves socked balls that rolled past the Westlock outfielders. The next two hitters walked, which forced in a run and loaded the bases. But, after throwing three balls outside the strike zone to the sixth hitter in the Braves lineup, Leon threw two strikes straight down the middle.

"All right, full count!" Mo cheered.

The next pitch came out of Leon's hand, and it was too high. It was at the hitter's eye height. But the batter swung. He chased the pitch and missed.

Two out!

Three Outs

The next hitter smacked a fly ball toward Marquis in centre field. He circled underneath the ball, just like before. But this time he flat-out missed the ball. It didn't even tick his glove before hitting the ground. Marquis picked up the ball and threw it back toward the infield. It soared over the head of Bobby Hu at second base. Mo backed up the play, but the ball scooted off his glove, bounced off his ankle and spun to a stop in the infield. By the time the ball was returned to the pitcher, three more runs were scored and the hitter had scampered as far as third base.

The next pitch, Leon threw over his catcher's head. The ball went to the backstop and the runner scored from third. The Braves had scored five runs so far in the first inning.

Then, the next batter swung and hit the ball toward Mo at shortstop. One hop. Two hops. Mo bent his knee and brought his glove down so the tip rested on the infield shale. The ball went into the pocket. Mo quickly rose from his crouch, transferring the ball to his throwing hand. Sonia was at first base. Her glove was the target. Mo fired the ball across the infield, and it was right on the money. Sonia squeezed the ball in her glove hand. Her foot grazed first base. The runner was still a step away from first.

"Out!" cried the umpire.

The Westlock players whooped and hollered and ran off the field.

"Guys, why are we celebrating?" Coach B. asked as the players got into the dugout.

"Don't you see?" said Mo. "We didn't give up seven. We actually got three outs. The inning wasn't mercied!"

And then Mo looked back toward his mom and dad. They were standing and cheering and high-fiving the Richards.

★ ★ ★

"Best game of the season," Mo beamed.

The team huddled in centre field after the game was called.

"But we lost again," said Coach B.

Coach Rau just shook his head.

"But we made it to the sixth inning for the first time," said Mo. "We even scored a couple of runs. We finally got past the minimum five innings without getting mercied."

"But we still got mercied," said Coach B.

"But not till the *sixth* inning," said Remi. He was nodding in agreement with Mo.

Coach B. shrugged. "So you guys are all saying that you feel good because you got mercied in the sixth inning instead of the fifth?"

"Yes!" cried the players all together.

"Look, the big Lloydminster tournament is coming

up," said Mo. "If we work hard enough, we might be able to get to the sixth inning again by the time that mercy rolls around. That would be awesome. I mean, Coach, this is exactly what you talked about, right? *Reachable* goals?"

Coach B. took his cap off. He scratched his head and then scratched it some more. "Well, maybe. I guess. Maybe."

17 Humbled by HUMBOLDT

Mo had never been to Lloydminster before. He thought whoever this Lloyd person was, it was awfully weird of him to launch a city that sits half in Alberta and half in Saskatchewan. Mo looked at the orange columns rising out of the ground in the middle of the city. They marked the border between the two provinces. The Legion Fields baseball complex was on the Saskatchewan side. Mo wondered why so many baseball fields were named "Legion" this and "Legion" that.

Near the diamonds was a trailer that served as a concession stand and tournament headquarters. Schedules were taped to the back of the trailer, listing the names of teams from across Alberta and Saskatchewan.

Westlock. Humboldt. Yorkton. Lloydminster. Edmonton Terwillegar. Strathmore. Grande Prairie.

Westlock's first game was against Humboldt, who had a starting pitcher who threw harder than anyone Mo had seen so far. But in the warm-ups, although the Humboldt pitcher threw awfully hard, he threw awfully wild. Only one of his warm-up pitches snapped neatly into the catcher's mitt. The others rattled off the backstop fence.

"Okay," Coach B. said as he gathered his team in the dugout. "Look at that pitcher. He might have a hard time throwing a strike. So I want you all to take pitches without swinging until you get a strike called on you. Let's see if we can grind out some walks."

Leon "Ball Magnet" LeMay raised his hand meekly. "But Coach, he throws so hard. I mean, I don't like to play against pitchers who throw hard like that."

The coach sighed and rubbed his eyes. "Leon, I hate to tell you this. But as you move on in rep baseball, you're only going to see pitchers who throw harder and harder. The point of the sport is to try to hit a ball off a pitcher who is throwing it as hard as he possibly can."

Leon's face scrunched up for a second. "I understand, Coach," he said.

The umpire called, "Play ball" and Remi walked up to the plate. He stood still as a statue, as the first pitch bounced before it got to the plate.

"Ball one," said the ump.

How come umpires always yell like they stub a toe when it's a strike, but you can barely hear them when it's a ball? wondered Mo.

The next pitch went a foot over Remi's head. The third and fourth went to the backstop.

"Take your base!" said the umpire.

The next two hitters walked on four pitches too.

Westlock had loaded the bases on twelve pitches, all of them balls. The Humboldt manager, dressed head to toe in blue, went to the mound to talk to his pitcher. He gave the pitcher a pat on the shoulder and then walked back to the dugout.

Leon was up. The first pitch came out of the pitcher's hand and roared through the zone.

"Strike one!"

Leon shook his head. But the next pitch was a foot outside.

The third pitch was right across the plate. But Leon didn't swing. He backed away from the plate instead.

"Come on, buddy, hang in there," Coach B. called from the third-base coaching box.

But Leon didn't hang in there. He ducked as the third strike screamed across the plate.

One out.

Sonia got her bat on one of the pitches, but it went foul. Mo was in the on-deck circle as she took two more swings and missed.

"Looks like the pitcher isn't wild anymore," came a voice from the Westlock bench.

"Okay, son," said Mo's dad from behind the backstop. "Just remember what we worked on. Relax. Quick swing. Easy swing. Eyes on the ball. Have fun."

The first pitch blazed across the plate in the blink of an eye after it left the pitcher's hand.

"Strike one!"

Relax, Mo thought.

The next pitch was a blur out of the pitcher's hand. But Mo could tell something wasn't right. The angle was all wrong. Wait, it was too high. Too far inside. *Duck!*

Then there was pain. It shot up from his shoulder blade and into his neck. Mo collapsed to the shale, not quite sure where the ball had hit him. He hurt from his arm up to his head. Mo rolled over once, twice, as the coaches ran in from their spots on the baselines.

He looked back to see that his dad was pressed up against the backstop fence.

"You okay, son?" his dad asked.

Mo put up a thumb, slowly.

The crowd members clapped.

Mo got up. "I'm okay," he told his coaches.

But the coaches asked the umpire if the team could bring in a pinch-runner for Mo.

The umpire nodded. "You have to put in your last out. So, that girl. She's got to go in for him."

Sonia walked to first base as the coaches helped Mo to the dugout. Remi's mom, who did first-aid, was waiting there for Mo. She rolled up his right sleeve so she could see his shoulder. It was already purple and yellow. She strapped an ice pack to Mo's shoulder.

"Are you sure you're okay?" she asked.

"No," said Mo. "I'm not."

Easy Out

★ ★ ★

It was the bottom of the fifth. Mo's arm was still throbbing. He had been put in left field to keep him from having to make a lot of throws.

Humboldt was up 11–4. Three more runs and they would be beating Westlock by ten. The game would be called.

There were a couple of outs, and Humboldt had runners on first and second. Bobby was on the mound. His first pitch sailed wide of the plate and rolled to the backstop, but the Humboldt runners couldn't run on the wild pitch. Because Humboldt had a seven-run lead, the only ways runners could advance were on walks, errors or hits.

It's bad enough we're down by seven, Mo thought. *But let's not get mercied. At least not yet.*

"Come on, two out!" yelled Marquis at shortstop. "Play at any base! Come on!"

The Humboldt hitter was left-handed, and Mo knew that Bobby didn't throw all that hard. It was likely that any hit would go to the right side of the diamond.

He won't be hitting it this way, he thought.

But he did. The Humboldt hitter took a hard swing and the ball went off the end of his bat. He got enough of the ball that it headed over Kaden's head at third base. But not enough so it would carry all the way to

Mo's spot in left field. So Mo ran as hard as he could.

Maybe, maybe I can get there, he thought.

The ball was sinking fast. Mo threw himself head-first toward the spot where he thought it was going to land. His glove hand was outstretched.

He felt his bruised shoulder burn as his arms hit the ground. The ball bounced and caught him in the chin. It rolled away.

"Go, go, *go!*" Humboldt's third-base coach yelled at his runners. With two out, they had taken off at the crack of the bat.

Mo got up and scrambled after the ball. The runner on second had already rounded third and was heading for home. The runner on first had rounded second and was going into third. The hitter had rounded first and was scooting toward second.

"Throw to the cut-off!" cried Coach B.

Marquis had Mo's spot at shortstop. Mo hoped to see him turn around to cut off the throw. But Marquis was rooted to his spot, mesmerized by the baserunners all around him.

So Mo threw toward third base. Would he get it there in time?

Kaden stretched out his glove to make the tag. The lead runner was still ten feet away.

If he catches the ball and makes the tag, that'll be out number three, Mo thought.

But Kaden didn't make the catch. The ball bounced

off his glove and toward the Humboldt dugout. It hit the fence next to the dugout entrance and stayed in play.

The runner from third scored to make it 13–4. The hitter sprinted from second, heading to the bag Kaden had left to chase the ball.

Panicked, Kaden threw the ball toward home plate. The ball sailed over the catcher's head. The runner from third came home to make it 14–4. And the game was over.

18 Summit in the BREAKFAST ROOM

The Westlock team had booked rooms in one of the travel hotels across the street from the diamond. The players, parents and coaches gathered in the lounge, which doubled as the spot to get free breakfast in the morning.

"That was a tough beginning," Coach B. said.

"We are getting killed," said one of the parents. "I'm not sure this is what we signed up for."

There were a few nods in agreement.

"Wait," said the coach. "I know you are all frustrated. But, in fact, it is what we all signed up for when we decided to restart the double-A program. We knew we might be biting off more than we could chew, and that's exactly how it turned out. And the kids keep reminding me of that, too."

"But look, we have some kids here who have potential . . ." said one parent.

"My kid isn't getting the chance to pitch . . ." cried another.

"You were on that big provincial championship

team. How come these kids aren't learning anything?" grumbled a third.

"*Enough!*" came a voice from the back of the room. It was Mo's dad. "Let's face it, these are kids. They're going to make mistakes. You may not see it, because you're all hung up on winning, but these kids have actually improved quite a bit. Start of the year, they were losing by twenty. Now it's ten. I didn't see it at first, but my son helped me. Joe, remember earlier this year, you talked about 'respect in sport' and having 'realistic expectations'? What happened to that?"

He drew a deep breath before he went on. "I see the problem. You're all frustrated because your kids aren't winning. You're mad because they were thrown to the wolves and haven't responded by winning and winning and winning. You know how I know? Because I was like that, too. I saw the games and I was angry. I wasn't thinking about what a big ask it was, expecting these kids who have never played double-A ball to all of a sudden go out there and beat the world. It took me a while to see my son wasn't having fun. It took me a while to see that, because something bad happened to me a long time ago. I was hoping my boy would pick up right where I left off. So let's lay off."

He sat down next to Mo. His son gave him a high-five.

"That was awesome," Mo whispered to his dad.

"Thanks, Big Mo," said Coach B. "And you're

right. I have let the whole 'realistic expectations' thing get away from me. You're not going to take a kid who struggles to hit a ball and turn him into a provincial team prospect in one season."

"Him or her," growled Sonia from another part of the room.

"Sorry, my bad. Him or her," said Coach B. "But we can maybe get a kid who was struggling at the start of the year to the point where he — or she — is making contact. Or catching a ball a little more regularly. We might not be winning, but we're improving. And that's the first thing."

He pointed to Big Mo and said,"We were pretty lucky, you and me. We played on a stacked team twenty-five years ago. But this is a totally different thing. A week ago the kids told me that their goal was to not get mercied till the sixth inning. I thought, 'That's crazy. What kind of goal is that?' But it dawned on me. It's a baby step. And one I think we can do. It's a reachable goal."

There was a cheer from the players in the room.

"Look, I think we have some good little ball players in this room," he went on. "And I think we can do that. In fact, maybe we don't get mercied in the fifth inning anymore!"

Another cheer.

And then it came out of Mo's mouth: "And then maybe we just *lose*! Maybe we don't get mercied at all and we play all seven innings!"

As the biggest cheer went up, a hotel staffer in a

black jacket and pants walked over from the lobby. He asked the team to keep it down, adding, "Wow, you must be doing so well at the big Lloyd tournament. You are all so excited!"

"Yes we are!" said Mo. "We're going to go out there — and not lose by *ten!*"

To celebrate Mo's announcement that Westlock was not going to lose by ten, Coach B. granted his team one hour on the waterslide. The sign on the hotel claimed it was "the FASTEST and LONGEST in all of Lloydminster!" The teammates hooted and hollered so loudly as they zipped down the slide their parents had to cover their ears. The sound of the screaming kids was like a jet engine and a heavy-metal concert mixed together.

★ ★ ★

The next morning, the families made the hundred-metre drive from the hotel parking lot to the baseball complex across the street. The street they had to cross was the Yellowhead Highway, and there were no sidewalks on either side of it. It was clear that the people who had planned the city didn't think anyone could get from place to place by walking. So it was actually safer to drive from parking lot to parking lot rather than take what should have been a three-minute walk from the hotel to diamond 2.

They arrived almost an hour and a half before game time.

19 Expect No MERCY

It was time to get down to business. The team gathered in the outfield of diamond 2. They jogged, then did butt-kickers and squats to get loose. The team followed Mo through a sequence of high leg kicks.

It was still early enough in the morning that the dew hadn't burned completely off the grass. Bugs scattered with each step the teammates took in the outfield.

The Westlock kids were in the dugout for their first water break when the other team arrived at the diamond, dressed in all-grey uniforms. Terwillegar.

"So, kids," the opposing coach said at the top of his lungs. "I looked at the Baseball Alberta schedule and standings. This Westlock team hasn't come *close* to beating anyone this year. I'd like this to be over in five innings, so I can save the pitching staff for *real* games against *real* teams later in the tournament. Let's go and kick their butts!"

"Classy," Remi said to Mo before gulping from his water bottle.

Coach B. walked into the dugout. He put his arms out, palms down, the sign that he wanted the team to gather. The Westlock kids circled their coach.

"All right," Coach B. said quietly. "I'm sure you just heard that out there. But we're not going to let them get in our heads. I don't want to hear any of you talking back or starting something with these guys. They think because they're a big bad Edmonton team, they can bully us. Let's just play the game with our heads held high."

The Westlock team followed their coach into the infield. The players took turns fielding ground balls. Coach Rau smacked the ball out to the different positions on the diamond. Mo cleanly fielded the first ball hit to him. Then he made a slow and careful toss to Remi, who was standing at first base. It was Mo's first throw across the diamond of the day. He didn't want it to be wild. Not with all the Terwillegar players staring at him.

"Wow, can you lob that any slower?" called one of the Terwillegar kids from their dugout. "Hey guys, if that's how they play infield, we can crawl to first!" And then there was laughter.

Sonia was the next to field a ground ball, and she reared back and fired a bullet across the diamond right toward Remi's glove. Just before the ball made contact with the leather, Remi's hand moved just a bit — enough that the ball went by. So it went screaming into Terwillegar's dugout.

It hit the bench with a mighty *crack*, sending the Terwillegar players scrambling. Remi looked over at Mo and, just for a second, flashed a smile. If Mo had blinked, he would have missed it.

"Hey, first baseman, *learn to catch the ball!*" screamed Terwillegar's coach.

"Sorry," Remi said. He put his hand up as an apology. "I'll do better next time."

★ ★ ★

"Okay, down five to nothing after half an inning," Coach B. said as the Westlock players ran in from the field. "We were able to get three outs, though. No seven-run mercy. So, good job, I guess?"

"Yup," Remi said as he threw down his glove. He traded his "W" cap for a black batting helmet. "I figure these guys are saving their best pitchers for other teams, so I think we can score here and there. If we can get three this inning, we'll only be down by two. If we lose every inning by only one or two, there's a good chance we can make it to the seventh. A full game!"

"I wonder what the seventh inning is like," said Sonia.

Remi walked out to the batter's box. The Terwillegar pitcher had just finished throwing his warm-up pitches.

Remi didn't wait long to swing. The first pitch came in over the plate at his knees. He made contact. The ball flew toward third base. It was fielded by the Terwillegar third baseman, but he had to make the long throw across the diamond before Remi got to first base.

Mo watched his best friend put his head down and run as hard as he could. He could hear the voices of Mr. and Mrs. Richard from the crowd.

"Go, Remi!"

The throw came across the diamond. It was going to be close. The first baseman leaned forward, leaving his foot in contact with the bag. The more he stretched, the quicker the ball would get to his glove. And the more likely that Remi would be out.

To Mo, it looked like Remi's foot hit the bag at the same time the ball hit the first baseman's glove.

Tie goes to the runner, Mo thought.

"Safe!" Mo heard his dad cry from the stands.

"Safe!" That was Mrs. Richard's shrill voice.

Then, the umpire extended his arms. *Safe!*

The Westlock parents clapped.

"Way to hustle, son!" Mrs. Richard called.

But just as Remi got a high-five from Coach Rau in the first-base coaching box, a figure came out of Terwillegar's dugout. He wore a black cap and a black training jacket. He took deep, wheezy breaths. His face was red as a tomato from Mo's mom's backyard garden.

"What was *that*?" Terwillegar's coach pointed to the umpire at first base. "*Safe?* Bull! You waited to make that call. You heard all those parents from the other side calling safe, and you let them make the call for you!"

The umpire looked away. "He got there in time," he said quietly.

Coach B. crossed into the diamond from his third-base coaching box. He spoke to the Terwillegar coach in a soothing voice. "Hey, the umpire is just a kid. He's doing his best."

"Easy for you to say. The call went your way!" cried Terwillegar's coach. "Are your fans going to continue to call the rest of the game for the ump?"

There was applause from the Terwillegar parents behind the first base dugout. They called out.

"Yeah, not only does your team suck, but you're also cheaters!"

"Let the ump do his job!"

"Cheats! I guess you have to do anything you can to even get a run."

Mo wanted to scream. *It was a close play. The Terwillegar team is already up by five. Why are they so angry?*

"Hey, guys, calm down," said Coach B. "These are just kids."

"No, these are *rep* kids!" cried Terwillegar's coach. "If you want to say, 'Be nice, these are just kids,' go and play house league! This is a big tournament. And we pay these umpires to call a good game."

"Oh, *shut up!*" cried Mo's dad from the stands. "What, are you scared because we got a base runner on? Can't handle it?"

The coach paused. "You know what, smart mouth? You're right. Go on, have the umpire on your side. We're going to smack you anyway. Look, I've been to your crappy little town once. Heck, I wouldn't even take a dump in it. That's how bad it is. We'll beat your nothing team from your nothing town."

And he turned around and walked back to his dugout.

20 Easy OUT

The bases were loaded. Remi was on third. Sonia on second. Mark Laboucaine on first. Two out. And it was Mo's turn at the plate.

"Go on son, relax. Have fun," his dad called from behind the backstop.

"Oh, Mr. Shut Up's kid is up," yelled one of the Terwillegar parents. "Why don't we shut up his kid by striking him out? Easy out, everyone. *Easy out!*"

"Time!" called Coach B. He walked over to Mo.

"They're just bullying us, trying to intimidate us," he whispered in Mo's ear. "You got that? Remember what I said. Play with your head held high."

The home-plate umpire walked up to Mo and Coach B. "Okay, let's play ball."

"Hey, how long are you going to let those guys talk to you and the other ump like that?" Coach B. asked the umpire.

"We'll deal with this." The umpire nodded and put on his mask.

"Hey!" called Terwillegar's coach from the dugout. "You talking about my team over there? Come on over here and say it to my face, or just shut your pie-hole!"

Coach B. shook his head and went back to the coaching box.

"Strike him out!" Mo heard as he stepped into the box. But through the yelling and chanting, he was able to pick out his dad's voice. "Have fun. Quick hands."

Mo closed his eyes. He took a quick breath but exhaled slowly. He took a practice swing and then got his bat ready, above his shoulder. The pitch came toward the plate.

Mo didn't feel the ball hit the bat. He just heard the loud ping off the aluminium. He didn't see where the ball was going. He could barely hear both of his coaches yelling at him to run. By the time he rounded first base, he could hear the cheers from the Westlock bench. He knew the ball was fair, somewhere.

"Come to third!" he heard Coach B. cry as he rounded second base. "Hard, hard, *hard!*" Coach B. urged Mo to run as fast as he could.

Mo huffed and puffed. He was getting closer and closer to third. He saw that the Terwillegar third baseman had put his glove out to catch a ball that could be coming in at any second.

"*Slide!*" cried Coach B.

Mo thrust one leg forward and tucked the other under his butt. The shale dug through his white baseball pants and tore at his skin. His foot hit the bag just before the tag.

"Safe!" cried the ump.

Coach B. patted Mo on the head. "Three-run triple, kid."

"None of this would have happened if you would have got that first out call right!" cried Terwillegar's coach.

And with that, the home-plate umpire cried, "That's enough!" He pointed at the Terwillegar coach, then put his thumb in the air. "There is someone who is out, after all! You are out of here!"

Terwillegar's coach had been thrown out of the game.

★ ★ ★

Coach B. gathered his team in the dugout.

"Okay, everyone, what's the score?"

"It's 10–5, Coach," said Sonia. Mo could see she was trying hard to keep her wide smile from erupting into a belly laugh.

"And what inning is it, everyone?"

"We're heading to the bottom of the sixth," said Mo.

"So what does that mean?"

"If we don't give up three runs, we have to play the seventh inning. We keep playing because there's a chance we can score seven in our final at bat and tie the game," said Remi. "We'll get to play an entire seven-inning game."

"That's right," nodded the coach. "Remi, you ready to go in and pitch?"

Remi nodded.

"Okay, let's go get them."

The players dashed to their positions. Mo took the shortstop's spot between second and third base. He and his infield teammates tossed the ball around the infield as Remi threw three straight warm-up pitches in a row over the catcher's head and to the backstop.

Mo approached the pitcher's mound and tapped his friend on the shoulder. "You can do this."

"It's a lot of pressure," whispered Remi. "I mean, we're so close to not being mercied. It's on me."

"No, it's on all of us. We'll make the plays behind you, you'll see."

Remi smiled. "This is insane. The shortstop of a team that hasn't come close to winning a game this year just told me that I should have faith in him and his team."

"Well, it's insane we're playing double-A ball in the first place!" Mo smiled, gave his friend one more pat on the shoulder and jogged back to his position.

Remi still had a smile on his face when he threw his first pitch, and it dropped across the plate.

"Strike one!" called the home-plate ump.

"This guy couldn't throw hard enough to break a pane of glass!" called one of the parents from behind Terwillegar's dugout. "Let's kill him and end this game! Faster we win, faster we can celebrate back at the hotel!"

The second pitch bounced before the plate. Ball one. The next pitch was popped high into the summer sky. Leon parked underneath it near first base, and the ball dropped nicely into his mitt. *One out!*

"Yeah!" cried Mo.

The Westlock fans behind the third-base dugout cheered.

"Can someone tell them that their kids are losing?" cried a Terwillegar parent.

The next batter took a mighty swing and the ball rocketed off the bat. It soared over Kaden's head at first base. Marquis in right field was way too far away to have any chance of making the catch. But the ball was hooking. As it kept flying, it headed off to the right.

The ball hit the ground about 150 feet from home plate. It was also about a foot on the wrong side of the right field line. Foul ball!

Remi closed his eyes and took a breath on the mound.

"Don't worry, Remi! Just a loud strike!" yelled Remi's mom.

The next pitch was hit just as hard. The Terwillegar bench erupted into cheers as soon as they heard the crack of the bat. But this time the ball was headed toward centre field, where Sonia was playing.

She stuck her glove hand into the air as she ran backward, turned around, backpedalled.

No way she catches this, thought Mo. *She's still only a beginner.*

But there it was. She fell forward as she squeezed her glove, as if the force of the ball was too much to handle. But the ball didn't roll out. It stayed put, in the pocket of her glove.

"Batter is out!" cried the umpire.

One out to go! Mo thought. *We can do this!*

But Remi threw eight balls in a row, none of them near the strike zone, walking two batters. The Terwillegar hitter at bat represented the run that could make it 13–5 and end the game early.

Coach B. asked the umpire for a time-out and walked to the pitcher's mound. Mo joined him there.

"Okay, Remi, just settle down," said the coach. "Play catch. Just like practice."

"You've got this," said Mo.

"All right, let's play ball," called the home-plate ump. Coach B. scurried back to the dugout and Mo went back to shortstop.

And Remi responded by throwing a pitch that was . . . close. But Mark Laboucaine, playing catcher, caught it cleanly in the mitt. Just like it hit the mark. And then he said, "Good pitch."

"Strike one!" called the umpire.

"No way!" cried a voice from the Terwillegar stands.

The next pitch was fouled back to the backstop. One strike to go!

"Come on, Remi!" cried Mo. "One more, no more! One more, no more! Play's to any base! Play is to the closet base!"

But this time, the pitch was greeted with the crack

of the bat. The ball flew into the outfield. The runner from second rounded third and scored.

11–5.

As Leon in left field ran to retrieve the ball, the Terwillegar cheering section erupted. "Go! Go! Go!"

The runner who had been at first came around third and headed for home.

12–5.

The ball was thrown to Remi, who had run to where the infield meets the outfield to cut off the ball. The hitter dashed from second to third. He didn't stop, but headed home in his quest to score the thirteenth run.

Remi had to make a perfect throw. He spun and tossed the ball to Mark, who stood at the plate. The runner was coming in fast. The ball hit Mark's glove just as the runner began the slide to the plate. Dust came up from the slide. Mark crouched as he reached down to tag the runner's lead foot . . .

"The runner's out!" cried the home-plate umpire.

"That's three out!" called Coach B.

A giant roar came from the Westlock parents.

"What?" cried Mo. "Did you see that? We're not going to be mercied!"

And before heading to the dugout, the Westlock players gathered near their on-deck circle. They piled on top of each other like it was the final pitch of the World Series.

Epilogue
SCREAMERS AND CELEBRATIONS

Mo's bike skidded to a halt in the parking lot of the Highway 44 Convenience Store and Gas Bar. Remi was only a couple of seconds behind, panting wildly as he came to a stop.

It was the hottest afternoon the summer had to offer.

The boys were hit by the welcome, cool blast of the air conditioner as soon as they opened the door. They each grabbed a large cup in front of the slush machine and began to fill up. Frozen bits of sour grape flavoured slush plopped into Remi's cup. Mo went for the orange-pop flavour.

The boys stopped pouring just before the cups got full. They moved to the ice cream machine to the left and topped off their slushes with soft-serve.

"So, a 'screamer' for each of you?" Mr. Speers asked as he adjusted his thick glasses behind the till. "Is that all?"

"Yup," said Mo as he and Remi moved to the cash

register. With his free hand, Mo began to rummage through his pocket for change.

But Mr. Speers put his arms out as if he was an umpire making a "safe" call. "No need that for that, local heroes. Your money is no good here today. This one's on me."

Remi smiled. "You know, Mr. Speers, I think I could get used to this local hero thing. Pretty good for a team that's only won one game all year."

Mr. Speers laughed. "It's not how many you win. It's who you beat!"

The boys nodded, said their thank-yous and walked back out to the parking lot. They sat on the curb to enjoy their screamers and watch the cars go by.

"So," said Remi. "Let's add up the score. Since that game, we got free burgers at the diner. Mr. Speers doesn't even want to see our money. And heck, I actually had someone ask me for an autograph at the rec centre."

"I was at the rec centre yesterday," Mo said after taking a deep suck on his straw. "And there's a team picture up there."

"I mean, I almost get this whole Barrhead thing, now," said Remi.

"Oof," said Mo. "I mean, we're still the worst team in Westlock history."

"But we didn't get mercied for five straight games before we played Barrhead," Remi said. "And we still have provincials to go. So who knows? Maybe we can even finish something like fifth or sixth in tier seven. As in, we won't be last in the province."

"Look," said Mo. "I'm still buzzing from this past weekend. We actually took the lead on Barrhead!"

And we kept holding on, Mo could see the thought run through Remi's head.

"So, it's 3–0, then 3–1, then 3–2. But Leon — oh, he told me he'd meet us later by the school. Anyway, Leon's pitching and Barrhead can't rally against him."

And then Mo ends up scoring the fourth run.

"So, not only is Barrhead not mercying us, but it's the bottom of the fifth. And we're up! And then it's my turn at bat. And *bang!* I hit a ball that goes right down the third-base line. By the time they fetch the ball, I'm on third. There are two outs. Coach B. tells me to be aggressive. The next pitch skips away from the catcher, not too far, but I go anyway. And the pitcher is charging in to cover the plate. And the catcher has the ball. And I'm still a long way from home. But I slide and the tag isn't there in time. I'm safe! We're up 4–2!"

But then Barrhead makes it 4–3.

"But top of the seventh inning, Barrhead's last at-bat, their first hitter sends a ball into the outfield. By the time we get the ball back in, it gets to 4–3. We have to switch our pitcher. Kaden, well, he comes in and walks two batters!"

And the triple play.

Screamers and Celebrations

Then a wild pitch moves them over. "Well, the next hitter hits a blooper. It looks for sure like it's going to go over my head and land in front of the outfielder. So the runners are going. But I run and run and jump and somehow I catch the ball. Now the runners have to scramble back. But I toss the ball to you over at third to get the second out. And you tag the runner who was going into third from second. Turns out he didn't even know I had caught the ball. Triple play! And we won our game!"

The only win so far.

"Sure, it's our only win all season. But we beat Barrhead. Barrhead!"

"Okay, stop," Remi laughed. "You know that I was there, right? Like, I don't need the play-by-play. But you keep telling me this story over and over. I think someone needs to ask themselves, who's just like his dad?"

"What?" asked Mo.

"Admit it," said Remi. "A few weeks ago, you're all, like, 'What's this big deal about Barrhead?' And now that we've beaten them, you're talking like it was the greatest game since the last World Series. Now who does that sound like?"

Mo went quiet. "Crap, you might be right."

"I know I'm right. But let's enjoy it. I mean, it's not often that the worst team in the world gets free screamers, right?"

ACKNOWLEDGEMENTS

Back in 1995, I was a reporter for the *Westlock News*. I covered the Westlock Legionnaires and the Westlock Red Lions. The Red Lions, managed by Chuck Keller, was the most-feared senior men's baseball team in the region. I covered their win of the North Central Alberta Baseball League championship. The Legionnaires were a true Cinderella story: they won the midget provincial championship after a so-so start to the season. True story: I promised to pay for a post-season party for the kids if they could upset a bunch of teams and win provincials. They made me pay up. And I drove one of the team floats in the post-victory parade.

When I lived there, Westlock was a baseball town. Baseball came first. It was a town that measured itself in balls and strikes. Baseball in Western Canada's prairies can be a very special thing. Summer afternoons lazily go by as local rivalries play out on the diamond. As you sit, hot dog in one hand, can of pop in the other.

A lot of this book was written in the spring and summer of 2019, in various hotel rooms in Alberta and Saskatchewan. My son played for the South Jasper AA Jays U11 Blue team, based out of West Edmonton. I was one of the assistant coaches. We played teams from across the province.

It was a special year and we had a great group of kids. So, to Tiny, Xavier, Big Kadin, Kenneth, Maddox,

Acknowledgements

Ryan, Blake, Adam, Poitras, Kehler and Tate, that year will be burned in my memory for a long time. Also, big shouts go out to Coach Derek "I Know Who You Are, Dr. Lampshire" and to Dallas, our other assistant coach. And to Yvonne, who made sure the umpires were paid and the hotels were booked. It's amazing how many people need to contribute for a team to thrive.

I learned a lot about rep baseball over that year. And nothing is more terrifying than throwing batting practice to kids who all hit the ball hard right back toward the pitcher. I felt like a human target. Thanks, guys.

Also, I have to thank my wife, Noelle, and my daughter, Nico, for coming along on the trip. It's not always easy sitting through a double header when you're nowhere near home. But there was that time the deer showed up in the playground behind the outfield fence in Okotoks. Right?

AUTHOR'S NOTE

The rules of junior baseball in Alberta differ a little from the Major League games you see on TV.

Pitch count: To keep young players from hurting their arms, no player is allowed to throw more than seventy pitches in a week. That means teams have to use a lot of pitchers over the course of their league and tournament games.

Length: Games are seven innings long.

Mercy rule, part 1: To keep scores from getting out of hand, teams are not allowed to score more than seven runs in an inning.

Mercy rule, part 2: If the losing team is behind by ten or more runs after it bats in the fifth inning, the game is called.

Mercy rule, part 3: Because the most you can score is seven runs in an inning, if the losing team is behind by eight or more runs after it bats in the sixth inning, the game is called.

Mercy rule, part 4: Once your team takes a lead of seven runs or more, you are no longer allowed to steal bases.